A Novel by the Residents of Arrow Senior Living

2nd Edition
© 2023 Arō Publishing

For the residents of Arrow Senior Living

Episode One

Cordelia Buttons had planned to sleep in. Let the med tech bang on the door, let the Resident Services Director chirp out her activity suggestions, it didn't matter. She would just ignore them. She just wanted to stay in bed and luxuriate in the feeling of her new soft pillows (purchased for $15.99 each) and 500-count sheets ($24.99). But what she hadn't counted on was Millicent Trueworthy, her best friend, calling at 6 a.m. to tell her that someone new was moving in. Someone...

"Very handsome from what I hear," Millicent said in a low voice. Millicent had been a smoker for 60 years, and even though Shady Bluff Senior Living was a no smoking community, she still found a way to smoke at least half a pack a day. Millicent thought all those cigarettes made her voice sound seductive. Cordelia thought she just sounded like a paper bag come to life. But Cordelia was intrigued, even if she had been pulled from a dream in which it was 2030 and Paul Anka was serenading her with *Diana* for her

90th birthday. He had still looked like he did when he sang it on TV back in '57.

"And he must be rich because he's a Count!" said Millicent.

"If he's so rich, Millicent, why is he moving to Shady Bluff?" asked Cordelia as she sat up. She wormed her toes over the floor in search of her slippers. "We are all very comfortable here, but it's not The Ritz."

Cordelia could practically hear the gears turning in Millicent's head. "Well, at any rate you know he's of good stock," she replied and sniffed in offense.

"I don't know what you mean by that, other than to imply some kind of snobbishness," Cordelia said. She had her opinions like everyone else, but she in no way considered herself a snob. "What did you say his name was?"

"His name," Millicent said, "is Count Dandy Caruthers." As if nature was conspiring with Millicent's preference for the dramatic, thunder crashed outside as she spoke the name. Positively villainous, thought Cordelia.

Cordelia considered herself to have something of a sixth sense about things: she could smell a secret or an opportunity from a mile away. It was she who realized it was cumin the cook was putting in the pizza sauce. She was also the one to figure out that if you convinced Housekeeping you saw a bug in your room, they would clean your apartment an extra time for free.

Something told Cordelia that this mysterious new Count was hiding something. And she was bound and determined to find it out.

Episode Two

It was Spirit Day at Shady Bluff: "The Awesome Eighties!" And while Cordelia wasn't normally the type for costumes, Millicent's enthusiasm was infectious.

Millicent announced herself by knocking 'Shave and a Haircut' on Cordelia's door. They appraised each other's outfits. "Look at us, all dolled up!" she said.

But Cordelia knew Millicent had other things on her mind. Sure enough, her thoughts were racing about the mysterious Count: is he moving here alone? Is he married? Does he have a girlfriend?

"I wonder what kind of woman he likes," Millicent said.

Cordelia laughed. "Well, if he likes 'em old and beautiful, you're certain to be a shoo-in for his girlfriend."

"If not, then he moved to the wrong place," said Millicent, lifting her head proudly. Cordelia told herself she better keep an eye on Millicent, who had a way of getting into trouble.

"Let's go to the front desk and see what we can get out of the receptionist," Millicent said.

The lobby of Shady Bluff was one of impeccable taste... if you ignored the '80s décor that the Resident Services Director had taped up on every possible surface. Cutouts of cassette tapes and boom boxes, sunglasses, *Back to the Future* movie posters... Cordelia thought it looked like a dorm room from 1986, which come to think of it, was probably exactly what the director was going for.

As they made their way to the front desk, the Executive Director, Regina Inkler, came out of her office and scowled, taking in the decorations.

Regina turned to them and her wrinkled forehead smoothed out, her eyes widened, and she gave them a big, gleaming smile with teeth that Cordelia was pretty sure were veneers.

"Don't you both look... festive!" she said.

Regina had not dressed for Spirit Day. She still wore her customary black dress and heels. Cordelia smiled, seeing herself and her best friend from the Executive Director's point of view: Millicent was wearing a bright, knee-length yellow dress, green and yellow bangle bracelets, and white strappy sandals.

"Millicent! What a shade of lipstick. I might just need sunglasses it's so bright!" Regina said, then she turned to Cordelia, who was wearing psychedelic, striped pants, a neon pink shirt, and a white sweater with a wide collar that dropped off one shoulder.

"Cordelia, you look positively... radioactive! I love that you got into Spirit Day! And look at those shoes!" Cordelia lifted a foot to better display her neon penny loafers.

"What are you ladies up to?" Regina asked as she began to rip the posters off the wall, muttering under her breath "If something is worth hanging," *rip...*, "it's worth framing," and she threw the poster into the trash can.

"We heard there was a new resident moving in?" Cordelia said.

Regina smiled. "Ah, I see what you are up to! No wonder you both are so *spirited*."

Cordelia waved away the implication. "You know how news travels. We were just curious. We hadn't seen a social profile." It was customary at Shady Bluff for new residents to share a social profile with the community so that everyone could better know their neighbor. But none had been received on the Count.

"The Count prefers to get to know people in person. If you want to know something, you'll have to ask him," the Executive Director said.

Millicent harumphed. "Sounds kinda shady to me," she said. Cordelia noticed the look that Regina gave Millicent for the very briefest of moments... Alarm? Fear?

"Well, you can talk to him yourself. He's due to arrive at any moment."

And sure enough, as she said this, a black limousine pulled under the porte cochère. The three ladies looked out the entrance as the chauffeur came around the car and opened the sleek black door. And out stepped the man himself... Count Dandy Caruthers.

Credits

Director... Sheila Gallagher
Writers... Dee Garcia
Isabell Gasser
Howard Simmons

Episode Three

All eyes were on the Count as he walked in. His lip curled on one side in cold amusement, and, under the lobby's chandelier, his monocle glinted like light catching on the side of a knife.

The automatic doors had just whispered shut when a loud scream erupted from inside the community. Standing in the hall between the dining room and the lobby was Shady Bluff's Executive Chef, Maxine Brûlée. Her face, normally a little red from cooking in the kitchen heat had gone pale with an almost ghostly green undertone. Her mouth was frozen open. *She's had a shock,* thought Cordelia, who glanced in the Count's direction and found him positively sneering as he looked toward the chef.

"What is wrong with you, Chef? That is not how we greet a new resident," exclaimed Regina, her admonishment ringed with warning laughter. She motioned as if to take the Count by his arm, but Caruthers deftly stepped aside so Regina's arm swept the air. To her credit, she continued the motion, so it looked to anyone but Cordelia's perceptive eye, as if she were waving him forward.

"I'd like to introduce two of your fellow residents, Cordelia and Millicent. And this is our Executive Chef, Maxine. She's exceptionally talented."

As the introductions were made, Cordelia noticed that the Count barely made eye contact with the Chef. If she hadn't caught him sneering before, Cordelia would have just blown it off as rude, but now alarm bells were going off in her head.

"Regina," said Maxine, her voice even smaller than normal. She seemed to be shaking. "Could we go talk privately? It's kind of urgent."

"Unfortunately, I have to get to a meeting. Count, would you like an escort to your room?"

"No, thank you," said the Count and his voice sounded to Cordelia like a snake slithering through the grass.

Millicent, however, didn't seem to mind. She had angled her left shoulder forward in a pose that she'd once confessed to Cordelia displayed all her best features.

"Count, would you please join the two of us for dinner tonight? We can show you around and fill you in on everything you need to know." Millicent smiled and batted her eyelashes.

The Count bowed his head, his lips tilting up just a little, in an approximation of a smile. "I appreciate the invitation, ladies, but I prefer my privacy and will be dining in my apartment this evening... alone. Quite lovely meeting you both," he said. Then turned, his cape snapping crisply as he did so.

Cordelia and Millicent watched him walk away, neither knowing what to think of all they'd just seen.

The next morning, around 5 a.m., before the day shift began and workers were too plentiful to dodge, Millicent snuck out for her first smoke of the day. She found it thrilling to do something illicit, as smoking was against the rules at Shady Bluff. She felt dangerous and exciting. As she entered the south stairwell, she heard someone making their way up, huffing at each stair. It was Count Caruthers and she rushed down, exclaiming, "Oh!" as she pretended to run into him.

But rather than seeming please, the Count looked almost terrified.

"Well, you are up early. I didn't peg you for an early bird," Millicent teased. "What are you up to at this time of day?" Millicent asked while primping her hair, ensuring it was perfectly set.

"I *am* an early riser. And I enjoy a good walk. It helps with the circulation," the Count said coolly. As he made to pass her, Millicent smiled and looked down.

"Oh no! You have a stain," she said and pointed to a red spot on his sleeve. "You know, a little baking soda and water scrub will take it right out."

The Count looked at the stain and then back to Millicent. It was like a light switch came on and he smiled, then winked. "Thank you, I'll give that a try," and, with a much swifter cadence, he continued his climb.

Cordelia and Millicent met up an hour later. Stride for stride, they made their way off the elevator and down the hall to the dining room, Millicent filling Cordelia in on the morning's meetings. They had volunteered to polish and roll silverware for Chef Brûlée, as there were so many other little tasks the servers had to do, and both Cordelia and Millicent liked helping the Chef, who was always so sweet.

Millicent told her about the Count's love of long, early morning walks and how he'd even winked at her. "He must be in need of a good woman, because he was walking around in a stained shirt, Cordelia. And you know I've always said how much I love doing laundry."

"You've never said any such thing," said Cordelia laughing.

They made their way to their favorite corner booth and set to rolling the silverware that Chef Brûlée had put out for them.

"It's awfully quiet," said Cordelia. There weren't any sounds of the normal bustle coming from the kitchen where the Chef was usually working to prep before her team came in.

They both waved as the first cook came in, yawning and stretching as he walked. The kitchen door made a little thump as it settled on it hinges. Cordelia and Millicent hadn't even rolled their first set of silverware before they heard the sound of pans hitting the floor and then the cook ran back out the door.

"Call 911! Call 911!" he shouted, waving his hands in the air. "Chef Maxine! She's... she's dead!"

Cordelia stood up and walked over. In his haste, the cook had forgotten that there was a phone in the kitchen. But Cordelia couldn't step in for as soon as she opened the door she saw Chef Maxine, leaning over a pot of tomato soup, but leaning too far, much too far... for her head was completely submerged in the pot of steaming liquid.

After the police came and took the poor Chef's body away and questioned the distraught cook and shaking residents, Cordelia and Millicent made their way back to their apartments, holding on to one another.

"To be drowned in tomato soup!" said Millicent, shaking her head. "That's no way to go."

Cordelia stopped, one hand coming to her mouth. "Millie, you said that when you saw the Count he had a stain on his sleeve?"

"Yes, just a little bit of red. I assumed it was blood from cutting himself shaving. You know men don't really notice those things."

"Was it blood? Or," Cordelia asked, staring at her friend, "could it have been tomato soup?"

Credits

Director... Abigail Smallwood
Writers... Donna Birdsong
Lorraine Johnson
Eleanor Stewart
Howard Simmons

Episode Four

It was strange how quickly things went back to normal at Shady Bluff that day. By the afternoon, events were continuing, and the halls were busy with residents going to and fro for appointments, meals, and scheduled events.

Neither Cordelia nor Millicent felt like participating. Cordelia wanted to be alone for a while and lay on her bed, thinking of the poor chef. She knew so little about Chef Brûlée. It made her sad to think that someone of whom she felt so fondly should feel like a stranger now. After all, someone had wanted to get the chef out of the way permanently. Had she known a deadly secret or had she something to hide?

Cordelia dozed off and was dreaming that she was running from a flood of tomato soup, when she was awoken by a knock.

"Who's there?" she asked, rising to a sitting position. The door opened and from the crack Pippi Footling, the community's Resident Services

Director, peeked in. Pippi's adorable, freckled face offered her a tentative smile.

"I'm sorry, Pippi," said Cordelia, shaking her head. "I'm not in the mood for yoga."

Pippi frowned, something Cordelia had only seen once before, during a particularly vicious round of cribbage. Her voice, normally a chipper squeak, shook. "I'm actually not here for yoga, Cordelia. I have my assistant leading today. I need to talk to you. Would you mind coming with me?"

As Cordelia stepped out into the hall, she noticed the concerned face of the Resident Services Director. Pippi's normal, perky façade had disappeared.

"Is this about Chef Maxine?" Cordelia asked, trying to communicate concern for poor Pippi, who really did look frazzled.

"No," Pippi said, "at least, I don't think so, but I need you to follow me." And Pippi immediately led the way, her long, red pigtails swaying vigorously. Pippi was moving much faster than Cordelia could and Cordelia suppressed a slight annoyance.

She guessed from the route that they were going to the garden, one of Cordelia and Pippi's favorite activities to do together. As they approached, Pippi started shaking her head. She crossed her arms in front of her protectively as she turned to Cordelia, nodding her head in the flower patch's direction.

"Look, Cordelia! The flowers. They're dead. Someone's destroyed them."

Cordelia hadn't noticed it as they approached, for dusk was settling over the community. But Pippi was right. A large swath of tulips were dead, their petals gone or blackened, the stems shrunken and twisted. And not only that, Cordelia noticed that the dead plants made a distinctive shape... that of a body.

Cordelia walked forward for a closer look. It really was getting dark out here... And as she moved, her foot caught on a raised root. She tumbled forward but landed softly on her side.

"Oh no, oh no!" shouted Pippi, who was thinking about the fall report she would now need to stay late to write. "Oh, Cordelia, are you okay?"

Cordelia wanted to tell her to stop fretting like some old hen, but she just said, "I'm fine, Pippi."

"Don't move!" Pippi yelled as Cordelia made to sit up. "We have to get your vitals. Lay exactly as you are." And she turned and ran back into the building.

Cordelia rolled her eyes. She was fine, but she lay back and sighed. What a day this had turned out to be. Her eyes moved to the flower bed. Through the healthy plants she could see the burned flowers she'd worked so hard to keep healthy.

Then, in the bed, nestled between the leaves and stems, she saw something white and square, with sharp edges. She reached out, her hand snaking between the tulips. It was a piece of paper, perhaps a note?

She opened it, straining to make out what it said in the twilight. There were splotches of some liquid: red ink? Or food? *Tomato soup?* Cordelia asked herself.

She gasped as she read the contents, then folded the note back up and slipped it in her pocket before Pippi returned with the nurse.

You have until midnight this Friday or else, the note had read.

It wasn't addressed to anyone, but Cordelia wondered if it was meant for her. After all, she was the only resident who worked in this part of the garden. But if it was for her, what did it mean? She had until midnight on Friday to do *what?* Today was Wednesday, whatever it was she had two days left. *Or else,* it read. Cordelia shuddered and hoped Pippi would return quickly. It was really awfully dark out here now and if someone approached her from anywhere but the door she and Pippi had come from, she wouldn't be able to see them. She was suddenly very afraid...

Credits

Director... Amanda Blood
Writers... Vicki Davis
Arlene Scott
Howard Simmons

Episode Five

"Oh, Cordelia!" Mallory Practiss, the Wellness Director, said as she helped Cordelia to her feet. Cordelia grimaced, pretending to need more assistance than she actually did. Mal was always so desperate to help that Cordelia felt bad telling her she could stand on her own.

"Let me take you back to your apartment," Mal said and together they walked down the halls.

"Thank you, Mal," Cordelia wheezed as Mal accidentally tightened the gait belt she'd left around Cordelia's waist.

"Oops!" said Mal as Cordelia grunted when the belt's teeth pinched her skin. "I'm just Miss Butterfingers today!"

"That's okay, Mal. I'm alright." Cordelia smiled. "But how are you doing? Isn't tomorrow the anniversary of...?"

"My husband's death?" Mal finished for her. "Yes, it is. Not a day goes by that I don't miss him, of course, but you know sometimes it's like he never really died. Like I can feel him watching me sometimes..." Mal trailed off, a far-away look in her eyes and Cordelia cleared her throat and patted Mal's shoulder.

"Well, as they say, time heals all wounds. But that doesn't mean they don't still ache every once in a while. I hope you have a good evening, Mal. Thank you for walking me to my room."

Cordelia was about to sit down and watch a rerun of Miss Marple when her phone rang. "Oh Cordelia, it's Millicent! Something awful's happened! Can you come over?" Cordelia thought her voice was funny, a bit deeper than normal, but perhaps that was because of how frightened she sounded.

Cordelia ran over to Millicent's apartment, fear gnawing at her belly. Millicent was her best friend. She didn't know what she would do if something bad happened to her...

But as she rounded the corner, she saw a large figure emerging from Millicent's apartment. Cordelia stopped and took a step back then peeked around the corner.

The figure was wearing all black, a monocle catching the light... The Count! His cape almost hid his hand as it deposited something in a vest pocket.

Then the Count looked both ways, but Cordelia must have been out of his line of sight because he didn't see her peering around the corner. The Count had been stooping slightly but now he straightened and went striding the opposite direction from where Cordelia hid.

When it was safe, Cordelia rounded the corner, shaking. What had the Count done to Millicent? If he harmed even one hair on her head... but no, Cordelia couldn't think like that.

She knocked rapidly on Millicent's door. Millicent opened it immediately, but instead of looking worried, her eyes shone, and she smiled.

"Millicent, what on earth is going on?" Cordelia asked, stepping into Millicent's apartment. She gasped when she saw the state of the room. "Oh, my goodness!"

"Oh, that? Yes, it's nothing to worry about," said Millicent, waving her hand as if the complete dishevelment of her personal space were nothing more than an annoying fly.

"What do you mean, Milly? Someone's ransacked your apartment!"

"Well, the Count helped me look through everything and nothing's been taken. Not the jewelry or my spending money, so whoever it was didn't find what they were looking for."

"Are you sure? You should at least call the executive director and let her know. We can't have people going into apartments and destroying the place!"

Cordelia was flabbergasted that Millicent could be taking this all so calmly. It was completely out of character.

"What was the Count doing over here?"

Millicent smiled and looked away. *Aha!* thought Cordelia.

"He was just thanking me for my cleaning tip. He said it got the stain right out of that shirt."

That stain could have been evidence, thought Cordelia, but she didn't say anything.

"He stopped by just to thank you for that?" Cordelia said.

"Well, no. Actually, he asked me to have dinner with him. At The Pale Horse." Millicent looked slightly embarrassed, but also proud. The Pale Horse was the independent living neighborhood's in-house pub, where residents could drink pints of beer, listen to live music, and play trivia games on certain nights. It was mostly for independent living residents; in assisted living, residents who wanted to go had to pay extra to eat there. For that reason, it was where people went for a celebration or maybe even for a date.

Cordelia's feelings were hurt. Before tonight, neither Millicent nor Cordelia had been to The Pale Horse and they'd promised each other they'd go together.

"Well, that does sound very nice," Cordelia said, trying to not let her feelings show. "How was dinner?"

"Oh, Cordelia. It was wonderful! The Count was so friendly. He's so smart and funny! We just laughed and laughed."

"But Milly, I don't understand. Why did you call me just minutes ago sounding so frightened?"

"What? Call you? I didn't call you!"

"Yes, you did. You said something terrible happened. And then I come over and your apartment's a mess and you don't seem to mind at all! All you can think about is the Count?"

"I don't know what you're talking about. I didn't call you. Let me handle my affairs as I see fit, Cordelia," Millicent said, and Cordelia almost stepped back in surprise. Why was Millicent talking to her like this?

"Is something wrong, Milly? Is there something you're not telling me?"

"Of course, not, Cordelia. Not everything is about you, you know? I should probably go to sleep now. Goodnight!"

And Millicent ushered Cordelia out the door, closing it a bit too forcefully, Cordelia thought.

What on earth is happening? Cordelia wondered. If the Count was with Millicent the whole time, then he couldn't have gone through Millicent's room... unless he was using Millicent as a cover... or there was someone helping him...

Credits

Director... Katie Tanner
Writers... Barb Feskanich
Betty Golden
Doris Hill
Betty Keane
Rosemarie Martinelli
Howard Simmons

Episode Six

Cordelia woke Thursday morning with a pit of dread deep in her belly. She didn't want to see Millicent. She was still upset from the way she'd been treated the night before.

But resolving not to let hurt feelings derail her from the mysteries afoot, she dressed and headed out of her apartment. Ignoring the grumbling of her stomach, she passed the dining room. Millicent was in their favorite corner booth, laughing as the Count was animatedly telling her a story. As Millicent wiped her eyes, the Count made eye contact with Cordelia and sneered. Positively *sneered* at her!

Cordelia lifted her chin and continued walking. As she entered the garden, the sky was blue and the air had a perfect Spring coolness. She closed her eyes and breathed in, taking solace in the fact that it was a beautiful day. *Things always turn out right in the end,* she told herself.

But when she opened her eyes, she found a face staring intently into hers from no more than four feet away. Percival Beauregard was looking at her dreamily, a slight smile on his lips. Cordelia could practically see little hearts floating around his head.

"Percival, good morning," she said, taking a step back.

"Cordelia, love of my life," Percival said, and took a step forward. "Why, I'd say you look happy to see me. Have you given any more thought to my suggestion of a romantic dinner?"

Cordelia put up her hands up to stop Percival from advancing any farther. "I'm very flattered, Percival. You know that, but I'm happy being single."

Percival laughed and stepped aside. "You are always playing hard to get, Cordelia Buttons. It makes my heart race and my palms sweat."

Sometimes I wish it would make that heart stop, thought Cordelia. A thought for which she immediately felt terrible. She didn't mean that. It was just that he was so aggressive. It was really off-putting.

She looked over and smiled forgivingly. Percival ran a hand over his bald head, which reflected the morning sun, and returned her smile, somewhat sheepishly, Cordelia was happy to note.

Perhaps he could be of some use, Cordelia thought. After all, Percival was a retired police officer. He might be a helpful in looking for clues.

She walked over to the tulips to show Percival what she and Pippi had found yesterday, but the entire flower bed had been dug up and all the remaining tulips removed.

"What's the matter, Cordelia?" Percival asked.

"Who dug up the flower bed?" she asked.

"Oh, Jimmy the landscaper was out here early this morning. He said most of the tulips were dead."

"He was right. Someone had burned up most of them."

"Why would anyone do that?" Percival asked.

"Why indeed. Maybe to send a warning?"

"A warning? To whom?"

"That's what I'd like to know. But it does seem strange that our poor chef was drowned in soup, and then mere hours later someone burns up the tulips Pippi and I worked so hard on."

"Are you implying that they did this as a warning to you?"

Cordelia shook her head. "I don't know." And she didn't. She couldn't think of anything that she knew or could have done to make someone want to threaten her, especially in such a vague way.

Tomorrow was Friday and if the threat was meant for her, she only had two days to figure the mystery out.

"Percival, you used to be a detective with the police force, right? What do you think of all this? Why would someone want to kill Chef Brûlée?"

"Why does anyone want to kill someone else? Sometimes for love or jealousy. Sometimes to hide something. Sometimes for revenge."

"But Chef Brûlée doesn't seem like the type anyone would want to kill for any of those reasons. She was so quiet and sweet," Cordelia said, and she found tears coming to her eyes.

"You never know about people, Cordelia. You trust too much. Maxine Brûlée had secrets, just as everyone else does."

"Like what?" Cordelia asked. She took the handkerchief that Percival offered and wiped her eyes.

"Like poisoning," Percival said, and Cordelia gawped.

"I don't believe it!"

"I shouldn't be telling you this, but you know how much I care about you, Cordelia. I could never keep a secret from you. There were rumors that the reason Chef Brûlée left her last position was because she'd been accused of poisoning her coworkers, putting small amounts of arsenic in the almond cakes she served. Not enough to be lethal, but enough to make some folks ill over a period of time."

"So, you think someone killed her for revenge?"

"Maybe," Percival said, looking over the garden and toward the fountain. "That's odd."

"What?" Cordelia asked, and walked with him toward the fountain, in which a few birds were twittering and splashing merrily, unaware of the dangers that seemed to be lurking everywhere in Shady Bluff.

"There's a gas cannister here. It's empty," Percival said, picking it up and shaking it lightly. "But Jimmy wasn't doing any work today that required using gasoline. Why would this be out here?"

Credits

Director... Sarah Ramusack
Writers... Betty Birch
Barbara Hanawalt
Violet Love
Hilda Woodfork
Howard Simmons

Episode Seven

In the Executive Director's office, Regina Inkler was having a very difficult conversation. She was sitting in her office chair in front of her laptop, clutching the receiver of her office phone.

"Who told you that? How could you know that?" Regina listened, then gasped. "You can't prove that! Who told you that? I demand you tell me now."

She squinted as if able to drill a hole into the opposite wall. Whatever she was hearing was making her very unhappy.

"Look, this wasn't the first time we've gotten into trouble because of that no good, meddling chef. But still, I don't know what you're trying to imply. I had nothing to do with that. I always said Maxine could be trusted. I always stood by her, even with rumors about her and her... her extra-curricular activities!"

Regina stood up and began pacing. She paid no mind to the phone receiver's cord as her back and forth caused it to begin winding around her, until she could only face the back wall. It was at this moment that someone opened the door very quietly and began to listen.

After the person on the other end of the line finished speaking, Regina stomped her foot. "No, absolutely not! I don't care what the Count says! Any information you receive comes straight to me, do you understand? Look what happened to Chef Brûlée. If we mess this up, we're dead meat!"

The line went dead and as it did so, she felt the presence of another person in the room. A shadow loomed, blocking the sunlight from the window and Regina, breaking into a cold sweat, turned as best she could without going through the necessary untangling needed to extricate herself from the phone cord.

"C... Count," she said. "What a lovely surprise. What brings you to my office?" She attempted a smile.

"I was concerned, Regina dear. I'd been hearing some rumors and wanted to talk before they got back to you. Who were you on the phone with?"

The Count took a step forward and Regina, despite herself, took a small step away. She did not want the Count to know he made her nervous.

"No one. A disgruntled family member," Regina said. "You know how they can get sometimes. But what rumors are you talking about?"

The Count shrugged and smiled. "Oh, some of the residents are saying that Millicent Trueworthy and I have fallen in love, at Millicent's prompting, I'm sure. I just wanted you to know that anything I do is ultimately for us, *you and me*. But now I wonder if you do know that?"

"What do you mean?" Regina asked, finally freeing herself from the cord. She smoothed her dress, then walked around the desk to the Count, where she placed a hand on his chest.

"It sounded like it was you who were angry with the family member," the Count said. "I don't think that's any way to talk to someone who has so much at stake in the life of their loved one, do you?"

The Count placed his hands on Regina's shoulder, his smile full of menace and warning. "Regina, dear. You're shaking. Are you okay?"

She nodded her head emphatically. How much had he heard? "Yes, yes. Of course. You're right. But we shouldn't talk about anything here. You never know who could be listening. Why don't we meet tonight around 9 p.m. at Downing Dumpf's Motel?

I'll be waiting at the bar." She leaned forward and gave the Count a kiss.

He smiled, bowed, then walked out of the office and shut the door.

"No matter what, this will all be over soon," Regina muttered to herself and opened the top drawer on her desk. Inside was a small pistol.

Credits

Director... Kaylin Miller
Writers... Lew Meeker
Howard Simmons

Episode Eight

As Cordelia and Percival discovered the empty gas cannister in the garden, and Regina spoke with the mysterious caller, Millicent sat in the Activities Room for the morning's cribbage game.

She loved cribbage and never missed an opportunity to play. Other residents made their way in, taking their seats at the tables. Most of them already had a partner. Millicent did too, usually. But this morning, the chair opposite her, the one Cordelia normally occupied, remained empty. This wasn't much of a surprise, given their evening spat.

She waved at Tina Testament, who was one of her best friends, apart from Cordelia. Normally, Tina had a little trouble finding a partner. Her wife, Patricia Jonie (most people referred to her as Jonie), refused to play with her. People always thought Tina was cheating. Most games in which Tina played ended with her winning and the other team fuming and accusing her of pulling a sly hand.

As Tina sat down, she ignored the wary glances of her opponents and began to make small talk. "It's a funny thing about the weather," scoffed Tina, "they're saying there's going to be a really bad cold snap. Maybe even snow!"

She looked across the room at Pippi, who was showing a table the latest dance that was all the rage on some app called TikTok. Doubtless she was going to try to get residents to do it later for a post. Tina shook her head. "I wonder if Pippi will make us all tramp out in the snow for her famous s'mores." Pippi wasn't content with just chocolate, marshmallow, and graham crackers. She was always trying to fancy it up so it would be Instagram-worthy. Last year she had them smearing on peanut butter and even whipped cream until the residents were left trying to eat a large, dripping mass of sweet goo. The housekeepers, who had to clean the residents' winter clothing, had grumbled about it for weeks.

"Did you hear about the flowers in the garden?" one of the opponents said. She was a sweet little woman, a little mousy. Tina couldn't remember her name.

"I did," she said. "It's funny, when Jonie and I were out walking the night before Chef Brûlée died, they were fine."

Millicent made a grim face as she counted her cards at the end of the play. "Fifteen two, fifteen four, fifteen six..." The other team watched with low spirits as Millicent moved the peg six spaces forward.

"Did you see anything, Millicent? I remember seeing you out there smoking," Tina gave a conspiratorial wink. "Do you think some of the ashes might have blown into the flower bed?"

Millicent swallowed thickly, then pushed her chair back. "I think I'm done playing for today," she said.

"Milly," Tina said, standing up and following her out. "I was just teasing you, you know that."

Millicent turned on her. "Tina, everyone says you're too smart for your own good. But sometimes you say very stupid things."

Tina blinked in surprise and took a step back.

Realizing how she sounded, Millicent softened and smiled an apology. "Tina, I didn't mean that. I'm just on edge right now. I just have... I just have a lot on my mind."

Tina nodded in acceptance of the apology, but she didn't follow Millicent any further. And, despite her words, Millicent's body language was telling another story. She really was upset with Tina. *So,* Tina thought, *Millicent is hiding something.*

In Millicent's room, the Count was making her his special drink. "Don't tell anyone I'm smuggling in something a bit stronger than table wine," the Count said, giving her a wink. Millicent took a sip, grimaced, then threw the rest back in one long swallow.

"That's the ticket," said the Count, whose smile widened ear to ear. *He looks like the cat who ate the canary,* thought Millicent. Despite its unpleasant taste, it had a calming effect, warming her as it made its way to her stomach. It also made her head feel a little funny. She looked at the Count, who was suddenly even more handsome than before. She looked down at her dress... the color! Her dress was the most beautiful shade of red she'd ever seen. Had it always looked this beautiful?

Millicent giggled, then looked around the room. Everything was so beautiful now that she'd put the room's contents back to where it should be. And the lights above her head, why they looked like stars they twinkled so much.

"What was in that drink?" Millicent asked, putting a hand to her forehead.

"It's my secret recipe," he said, then sat beside her on the bed.

"Oh, Count. Thank God we've found each other. I don't know what I'd do without you right now. I'm so scared."

They held each other for a while, then the Count got up to make her another drink. "I don't think I should," Millicent said.

"It's good for you," the Count said. And as Millicent took a sip, he tipped the bottom up, causing her to splutter as she drank.

"Good, very good," said the Count.

"Now, tell me what happened this morning that upset you so much."

But Millicent was having a hard time putting her thoughts together. Those drinks Count Dandy was making. They made her feel good, but the more she had the funnier she felt.

She told the Count the best she could about Tina letting it slip to others that she still smoked and Tina's implication that Millicent might have started the fire in the flower bed. The flowers were Cordelia's pride and joy, and Millicent was already fighting with Cordelia. If Cordelia thought that she'd burned her flowers, she would be so angry.

"But I did see something," Millicent said. Through her distorted senses, she tried to remember what it had been. "I waited until all the lights were out and had just one more cigarette before bed. I remember seeing," and Millicent reached a hand out as if she could pull the memory from the air. "Something in the sky... It was green... like a UFO. Yes, in the sky, green and flying over my head and it was raining down little grains of pollen into the flower bed..."

The Count tried not to laugh. Boy, this drink sure did make people loopy. But soon enough it would serve his purpose and he would have everything he ever wanted.

"Don't think about it, Millicent, my sweet," he said and kissed her forehead, then her cheeks. "Whatever it was, I won't tell a soul."

"Oh, Count," Millicent said, and sighed.

As the day turned to night, the Count left Millicent's room, went down the halls to the exit closest to where he'd parked his car. He momentarily longed for his chauffeur back, but it was okay. Fernando would be back in his employment soon enough.

As he buckled his seat belt, he thought of Millicent's kisses and Regina's kisses soon to come. He was a very lucky man. He cast a glance back at the community. Behind the building, about where he supposed the garden was, there was an eerie glow emanating.

How very odd, the Count thought. And he pulled out of the parking lot.

Credits

Director... Andie Blood
Production Designer... Scott Harrison
Writers... Gladys Chirakos
Lois Davis
Berri Mushrush
Judy Wolfe
Howard Simmons

Episode Nine

Friday morning came very early for Cordelia. Sleep had eluded her as her thoughts raced... Millicent's strange behavior, the mysterious Count's arrival, Percival's puppy-dog look as he followed her around everywhere... But the thought that continued to surface above all the others was about the garden. What did it mean, the gas cannister, the note, the dead flowers in the shape of a body...? The more she thought about it, the more she wondered if it was all connected *or*... could this be a bit of misdirection to send her down the wrong path, to distract her from something much bigger going on at Shady Bluff?

Every Friday at Shady Bluff was French Pastry Day, when the private dining area usually reserved for small parties or events was transformed into a French patisserie. The day before the room was transformed into a banquet of delectable confections, Chef Brûlée would come alive as she prepared. The bakery was her baby, everything made from scratch and all the recipes secret, developed during her studies at an école culinaire in France. But that was as much information as she would give, anytime the conversation turned to her time in France, her brow would furrow and she would seem to close off to the world, excusing herself and retreating to the kitchen.

Cordelia frowned, resigning herself to a cup of coffee and whatever else might be offered to the early birds. As she neared the private dining room, she saw that the Human Resources Director, Herman Usurpera, was sitting inside. Cordelia tapped lightly on the French doors, unsure if he wanted to remain alone or not. Herman motioned her to come in.

He smiled. "Well, you are a beautiful sight on this somber Friday morning, Delia." Cordelia blushed. Even though Herman could have been her son, she was always quite flattered when he called her Delia.

She had to admit she'd had a little crush on him for some time now. In fact, who wouldn't? He was so darn handsome, and that tall athletic build also reminded her of her late husband, Nathan.

"I hope I'm not interrupting you," Cordelia spoke softly.

"Not at all, I'm just reflecting a bit on the week, and about Maxine, of course. Such a sad loss for all of us, but I'm so proud that, in her honor, her staff is putting together the bakery today as best they can.

She was so private, but she still made such am impact on those who worked for her. And, of course, the residents."

Herman seemed lost in thought for a moment, then snapped out of it. "No more reminiscing for now, I'm off to do payroll. I need to have everything done by noon so that I can work on the famous Shady Bluff Pickleball Classic! If you want to come by this afternoon and get the items for your Alzheimer's Donation Booth, I will be in event mode!"

Cordelia watched him walk away. There were so many things she didn't know about Herman, yet she felt closer to him than to most of the residents. He always had an open-door policy and never seemed to mind when she came in to chat. She treasured her time on the Alzheimer's committee with him, not just because he was so handsome but because he really had a passion and drive to give back to others.

When the first pastries were put out, she grabbed one and a cup of coffee and made her way to the courtyard and to sit in the garden. As she walked among the plants and flowers, being careful not to look at the empty space where her tulips once flourished, she made her way to the gazebo. As the community's space opened out onto the Perfidy Cliffs and the sea beyond, something in the back parking lot caught her eye. It was a black limo.

What in the world is a limo doing at Shady Bluff at 6 a.m.? A few moments later, she saw none other than the Count exit the community through the employee entrance. He was walking very quickly and with much more strength than when he walked around the community. He always seemed to have a slight limp, but not this morning; he was practically race walking to the limo. He was clutching a small suitcase to his chest. As he got into the limo, Cordelia saw something catch the light as it fell from his coat pocket to the pavement: the Count's keys! The Count didn't notice he'd lost anything, and the limo sped off to its destination.

Cordelia could not get to the keys fast enough. Her heart racing, she put them in her pocket and made her way back into the community. It was too good an opportunity to pass up.

Shady Bluff was a very quiet community early in the morning. Members of the staff were arriving for their shifts, but the few she saw were busy helping residents get ready for the day or being briefed on the previous shift's progress and any incidents that might have happened. She knew what she was about to do could get her in a lot of trouble, but she simply could not stop herself as she made her way to the Count's room and slid the key into the door.

She slipped right in without being seen, or so she thought. *I'll just leave the keys in his room when I leave. He'll think he just forgot them.*

The Count's apartment was very bare. *It looks more like a hotel room,* she thought. There were no personal items anywhere, just a few pieces of clothing, snack food wrappers, a few bottles of wine, and lots of cords. *Why does he have all these cords? How many devices does one person need?* she thought. She followed the cords from the wall to the closet. The door was closed, the cords snaking underneath. She put her hand on the closet door. It was warm, as if there were quite a bit of heat being generated inside.

As she started to open the door, the crack revealing a cold, green light from within, she heard a rattle from behind her, the squeaking of hinges, and the door to the Count's apartment opened.

Credits

Director... Kayleen Daughrity
Casting Director... Vicki Barnard
Writers... Cindy Meikel
Brenda Nelson
Steve Owens
Howard Simmons

Episode Ten

As Cordelia was watching the Count drive away, the Directors of Shady Bluff Senior Living were getting impatient. Their weekly department head meeting was supposed to start promptly at 8 a.m. Their Executive Director, Regina Inkler, demanded punctuality of all her employees. And yet here they were, twiddling their thumbs, waiting for *her!*

"I'm just about to go back and get started on the plumbing repairs to the east wing's bathroom," the Plant Operations Director said.

"I still can't believe it flooded our resident records room. The state is going to have a fit when they hear all our resident and employee records were destroyed by a flood from an upstairs toilet," said Herman Usurpera, the Human Resources Director, who was right to be nervous, because, while he loved her, Regina would no doubt throw him under the bus, so to speak, if needed, to save her own neck.

"Oh, I hope something hasn't happened," said the Resident Services Director, Pippi, who was wringing her hands so hard her knuckles were white. "Did I tell you that I overheard her talking to..."

But Pippi didn't get another word out, as the door suddenly burst open and the landscaper, Jimmy Steele, burst in. He flushed as everyone turned to stare at him. Pippi took a moment to admire the way his shirt clung to his muscles and one lock of his blond hair had escaped his baseball cap and hung over his forehead. *Stop swooning, Pippi,* she told herself.

"Haven't you heard?" asked Jimmy. "There's some woman demanding *loudly* to see Regina and the receptionist is practically in tears because she won't take no for an answer.

Someone was upset? Well, Pippi liked a challenge. She stood up and followed Jimmy to the lobby, admiring his broad shoulders, his slim waist... *Get a grip, Pippi!* Pippi chided herself. *Honestly, what is wrong with me?*

Pippi, despite her usually chipper demeanor and 'won't take no for an answer' attitude, was immediately cowed by the woman standing in the lobby. She was tall, probably six foot, with hair as dark and shiny as onyx. Her makeup was flawless on her already smooth, olive skin. Her lips, plumped and blood red, pulled back in a smile that closely resembled a shark's. Her eyes were hidden behind a very large, very dark pair of sunglasses, but, as the woman was a good foot taller, and she made use of her height by tilting her head down toward Pippi, like she would a child. Or a mouse.

"Surely, you're not her?" the woman said, her voice dripping with disdain.

"My name's Pippi..."

"I don't *care* what *your* name is. I want to speak to the person who runs this place. Or am I to assume that everyone is free to run amok here? Is there no order to the way you do business?"

"Regina is, um, out at the moment," Pippi said, doing her best not to flee in terror.

"Then I would like to speak to my husband. *Immediately!*" the woman didn't scream, but her voice rose and carried so far that it was as if she had.

"And who is your husband?" Pippi asked.

"Count Dandy Caruthers," the woman said. "I am his wife, Countess Lily Rose Caruthers."

Pippi looked at the receptionist, who picked up the phone and dialed the number to the Count's apartment. Her hand was shaking as she held the receiver.

"There... there's no answer," said the receptionist, who then burst into tears.

"That's okay, Rebecca," said Pippi. She turned to the Countess, "It would appear he is out as well."

The Countess drew herself up and breathed in and out very slowly. "Then, take me to his room, you *moron,*" she said.

"Everything okay?" came a voice from behind them. They turned to see Percival Beauregard standing in the entrance to the dining room.

"Yes, thank you, Percival. This is Countess Lily Rose. She's Count Dandy's wife. I was about to take her to his room."

"I'll take her," he said. "I know you're busy." And he looked at Jimmy and then at Pippi and winked. Pippi wanted to melt into the floor.

"Thank you, Percival. That's so sweet."

"Follow me," Percival said to the Countess. He didn't seem bothered in the least by her haughty manner.

When they were around the corner, Pippi let out a sigh. "I never thought I'd say this, but I feel sorry for the Count!" She smiled at Rebecca who, still smarting from the visitor's verbal lashes, burst into a fresh torrent of tears.

The elevator opened and Percival, normally prone to chivalry, stepped out first, cutting off the Countess. As she stepped out, her heel caught on the elevator door's track and she stumbled, the contents of her purse spilling. Before Percival could reach down to help, she'd scooped everything up. But not before he saw the gleam of a small pistol.

"My apologies," he said, smiling.

"Don't I know you from somewhere?" she asked, removing her sunglasses. Her eyes were golden, her gaze penetrating.

"Me? I don't see how, I've never hobnobbed with the rich and the famous before," Percival said.

"That doesn't surprise me," the Countess said, putting the sunglasses back on. "Still, I could swear I know you."

Percival, his pulse quickening began to sweat. Could his cover be blown so soon? But the Countess said nothing else, and he stopped at the Count's door. "I imagine that you have a key, since he's your husband," Percival said.

"No need," she replied, turning the knob. "It looks to be unlocked." The Countess stepped into the apartment, turned to face Percival, and slammed the door in his face.

"Troglodyte," she whispered, then let out a breath. "Ugh, this is where you choose to hide, Dandy?" She surveyed the room, then sat on the edge of the bed. She took off her glasses and massaged the bridge of her nose. "It won't be easy, Lily," she said to herself. "But it must be done."

A knock came from the other side of the door. Upon opening it, she saw Jimmy the landscaper on the other side.

"Hurry up, get inside!

Jimmy stepped in, closing the door behind him. He leaned against the door. "What are you doing here, Lily? My mom isn't here."

"Stop talking so loud. You shouldn't even be up here. You're going to spoil our plan. I didn't break you out of jail for nothing, Brexton."

"Don't call me that. My name's Jimmy. I'm starting a new life."

"I can call you whatever I want. You *owe* me." The Countess opened her purse and pulled out her lipstick. The gleam of metal caught Jimmy's eye and he stepped forward. "You have to do what I say. We made a deal: you help me get my husband back and figure out what his new *friend* is hiding and then you'll be free. But no one is going to get in my way, and that includes your mother." She closed the purse with a snap and then patted its side.

"What's in there?" Jimmy asked.

"A solution," she said.

Credits

Director... Kylie Hiatt
Writers... Marian Applegate
Jean Haskins
Glorine Knoerzer
Howard Simmons

Episode Eleven

Percival rode the elevator back to the main floor. Decades on the police force had given him a very keen sense of danger and right now alarm bells were ringing very loudly in his head.

Chef Maxine was dead, Regina Inkler hadn't shown up for work, and Cordelia's flowers had been burned in the shape of a body... it didn't seem a coincidence that after Pippi showed Cordelia the damage, Jimmy suddenly arrives to dig them up.

Poor Jimmy. *What a dumb kid,* thought Percival. To break out of prison only to return to Chance County. To be near his mother, Percival assumed. The only reason he hadn't turned in Jimmy, aka Brexton Inkler, was because he was certain Jimmy might come in useful later.

What no one knew at Shady Bluff was that Percival, while technically retired, had agreed to move into the community at the request of the County Commissioner, who was certain that something bad was going on here. Black SUVs seen pulling up to the employee entrance at the middle of the night. The strange green glow that some folks in town had reported seeing around the community and Perfidy Cliffs. Percival didn't know how all of it connected with the chef's murder and the sudden appearance of the Count, and now the Count's wife, but he was sure it was connected somehow.

Percival arrived at the HR Director's office and knocked on the door. Herman was sitting at his desk, fingers smashing away at the keyboard. Herman looked up and smiled. A genuine smile, Percival knew, not the smarmy, flirty one he put on for most of the ladies. How they didn't see through that, Percival wasn't sure, but he figured it might have to do something with how handsome Herman was.

Percival felt a pang of jealousy. He'd seen how Cordelia blushed when she spoke to Herman. He fervently wished just once that Cordelia would look at him that way...

"What's up, Percival?" Herman asked.

"You missed all the drama with Her Highness," Percival said, taking a seat in front of the desk. "The Count's wife made a very grand entrance."

"So Pippi said. It took us quite a while to get Rebecca calmed down. I'm guessing you left her up in the Count's apartment?"

"Yes. Let's hope she stays there, or you might have a mass exodus of residents on your hands. She doesn't seem like the type who wants to make friends," Percival said, chuckling.

"Was there something I could do for you? I'm happy to talk but as you can see, I'm a bit busy," Herman said, indicating the mounds of paperwork on his desk.

"I won't keep you long," Percival said. "I was just wondering if we could maybe say a few words in Chef Brûlée's honor today. Maybe call everyone to the bakery at the end of the morning?"

Herman nodded and Percival was surprised to see tears in the man's eyes.

"That's very good of you, Percival," he said, then cleared his throat. "Please forgive me. It's been a bit hard. I keep wondering…"

"Wondering what?"

"If there was something I should have done. If I could have protected her in some way."

"How so? From what I hear Chef Maxine didn't have any enemies," Percival lied. He knew that there were rumors Chef Maxine had poisoned her previous employer.

"Percival, I know I shouldn't tell you this, but I need to confide in someone. And it seems so many people have an agenda here, everyone's hiding something. But you, a retired cop, well, I can't help but feel you tell it like it is without any tricks or games."

Percival shifted in his chair, feeling a little guilty for his lie about the chef.

"Maxine and I were having an affair. Back when I was married, before my wife... Well, you know?" Herman said. "Sometimes Maxine would get so nervous, especially when we were out in public. I just assumed it was because she didn't want us to get caught.

"After my wife died, I felt so guilty for being unfaithful that I cut things off with Maxine, but then she got, well... obsessed. She called me up one night claiming she'd cut herself and needed me to take her to the hospital, but when I got there, she was fine. She started calling my phone at all hours and leaving messages..."

Percival studied Herman as he talked. He had spent years getting confessions out of the bad guys. His secret was just to sit there and listen. Most people wanted to talk if you were quiet enough, open enough to what they had to say.

"And then the night before she died, she called me, told me that she was afraid something was going to happen to her. She said she had noticed that I was falling in love with Regina, but that Regina wasn't to be trusted. Then she said she knew about Regina's secret, had proof. Something about the Count. But by then she was getting herself worked up. I thought she was lying."

"Chef Maxine getting worked up? She always seemed so cool and reserved," Percival said.

"Yes, most of the time she was. But no one knew her like I knew her. She was so passionate at times. In many ways. And that night, well, all her energy was focused on making me believe that she was in a lot of danger. But I didn't believe her, so I hung up on her. And then, the next day, she was dead."

Herman covered his face with his hands. He took several deep breaths, then brought his hands down and looked at Percival. "I'm so sorry, Percival. I shouldn't burden you with all of this. It's not professional."

"Oh, forget professionalism, Herman. We're friends, right?" Percival asked. Herman nodded.

"Did she say anything else? Tell you what kind of proof? Or where she might have kept it?"

Herman thought a moment, "She said something about documentation and the hospital.

And then she said if Regina had paid up when she had the chance Maxine wouldn't even be here."

"She was trying to get money from Regina," Percival said. "But why? What would Regina want to hide so badly that Maxine was blackmailing her?"

"I don't know, Percival. But she did say one more thing that I didn't remember until now."

Percival leaned forward.

"She said," Herman said, 'Millicent should have known better. If something happens to me, she should watch out.'"

Percival sat back, stunned. *Millicent?* How was she wrapped up in all of this?

Credits

Director... Mindy Miller
Writers... Norma Nagy
Beatrice Wilson
Howard Simmons

Episode Twelve

With Regina still AWOL, Pippi decided to take charge of running the day's operations. *Lord knows, Herman would just hide in his office all day, pretending to do payroll,* she thought.

After the front desk had calmed down from the Countess' arrival, Pippi made her way back to the Wellness office. If Shady Bluff was getting a new, unexpected resident, the Countess would need to have a care assessment just like everyone else. Pippi felt a pang of pity for the Wellness Director, Mallory Practiss. There was no way that haughty thing would like Mal or a nurse asking her personal questions.

As she neared the Wellness Director's office, she heard the director talking to herself. Mal was pacing around her desk, every other step punctuated by her limp. "What can it mean?" Mal was muttering.

Pippi stepped forward and knocked on the doorjamb. "Mal, hey. Is everything alright?"

Mal looked up. For a moment, her face was fearful. But then she gave Pippi a small smile.

"Sometimes, I wonder if I'm going crazy, Pippi," she said. "Or someone is trying to drive me there."

"Why? What's going on?"

Mal sat in her office chair. Her shoulders slumped and she opened a drawer. Pippi could see that it was full of little pieces of paper. Mal grabbed a handful and tossed them on the desk.

"I've been getting these notes. Ever since Richard died... right before any special occasion that we used to share, birthdays, holidays, our anniversary, things like that, someone's been leaving me notes. But on this year's anniversary of Richard's accident, nothing came."

"May I?" Pippi asked. She reached out and plucked a note. Read it, then picked up another. She slowly went through all of the notes on the desk. They were all strange and vaguely sinister.

Roses are red, violets are blue. You killed your husband, will it kill you?

and

Cash that check or you'll regret the day/ You cut the brake line, I have to say!

and

The payoff is fat, my greed is too/ You'll cash that check if you know what's good for you!

"Have you gone to the police?" Pippi asked.

"I did at first, but they couldn't trace where they were from and after a couple of years passed and nothing happened..."

"Oh, Mal, I'm so sorry. Do you have any idea who might have sent you these?"

"I wasn't sure, but now I think I do. I couldn't believe it at first, but the other night when I went to help Cordelia after she fell in the garden... Well, as I was helping her up, I saw her put a piece of paper in her pocket. It bothered me for a reason I couldn't quite put my finger on initially. But then she said something that I can now only attribute as being quite sinister. She asked me about Thursday, which was the anniversary of my husband's death."

"How is that sinister?" Pippi asked. "Cordelia's always so good about remembering things. She was surely just worried about you."

"Yes, that's what I assumed too, but then I thought back to that piece of paper she had clutched in her hand. It was a particular shade of cornflower. Not very common in stationery." Mal extended her hand, gesturing toward the notes on the desk. "But as you can see, whoever has been sending me these notes uses the same kind."

Pippi gasped, realizing what Mal was suggesting.

Mal, noting that Pippi was on the same wavelength as her, nodded her head. "Yes, I think these notes and threats have been coming from our favorite resident, Cordelia Buttons!"

Credits

Director... Katie Metzger
Writers... Carolyn Ballou
Audrey Bashian
Betty Daly
Ed Seegull
Howard Simmons

Episode Thirteen

Tina and her wife, Jonie, knocked on Millicent's door. It was 8:30 a.m. and Jonie had suggested she should invite Millicent to breakfast to smooth out their argument at yesterday's cribbage game.

"You're right, of course," Tina said, "And it would be nice to see what she's hiding."

"Don't say such things about your friends, Tina," chided Jonie, who always believed the best of everyone. "There has to be a reasonable explanation. I'm sure she'll tell us."

When Millicent opened the door, she looked completely out of sorts. They'd never seen Millicent without her makeup, perfect hair, and impeccable fashion, so they both stared aghast at her now.

"I must look something awful, the way you two are gawping at me," Millicent said.

"You just look a little tired, is all," said Jonie. "Are you not feeling well?"

"Oh, I'm doing alright. Just have a little headache." Millicent, seeing that Tina and Jonie weren't going to leave, smiled and said, "Would you like to come in?"

The ladies accepted the offer and walked into Millicent's apartment. "Please don't mind the mess," Millicent said. "I had the Count over yesterday and I guess we had a little too much fun."

"That might explain the headache," Tina said, indicating an empty bottle on the floor.

Millicent laughed mirthlessly, "Nothing gets by you, Tina."

"So, you like him, The Count?" Jonie asked, giving Tina a warning look that reminded her they were there to make up with Millicent, not get into another fight.

"Oh, yes. He's so charming and complimentary. I'd helped him with a stain and the way he went on about it!"

"Did he tell you why he moved here? I mean, a Count of all people, moving to our little community...," said Tina.

"Not really, although it turns out he knows Regina."

"Really? How are they are acquainted?" asked Jonie.

"I'm not sure, I think he was embarrassed after he mentioned it. I assume he didn't want me to think he was name-dropping. But of course, a Count would know everyone, wouldn't they?"

"Yes, I guess they would," said Jonie.

"Well, I have to say if Regina's friends with a Count, it would explain why she keeps looking at him so affectionately," said Tina.

"Yes, I noticed that too. But he doesn't seem to reciprocate," sniffed Millicent. "During our dinner date he held my hand while we sipped our wine. And he kissed my hand when we parted."

"Not to mention all the fun you must have had yesterday," Tina said, winking. "Ramona in apartment 23B said he was in your apartment for most of the day."

Millicent frowned. "You know, I can't quite remember yesterday. I only had a couple of drinks, but the Count sure does make them strong. I had to practically throw them back. I think the sugar cubes he used were stale or something. They were a little bitter."

Millicent laughed. "I haven't been that loopy from a drink since my sorority days. I was even seeing things: colors looked funny, everything was a little off. The Count sure teased me. I remember him pretending to look through my things for my sanity. He would open up a drawer and say, 'Where's

Millicent's sane deposit tea? Where would Millicent hide her sane deposit tea?'"

"Why would he be calling your sanity that? That's awfully strange," said Jonie.

Tina was quiet for a moment, thinking. Bitter sugar cubes. Odd colors. Could the Count have drugged Millicent? Her eyes widened. Was it LSD he'd put in her drink? But why? Tina gasped.

"Millicent, do you think he might have been saying safe deposit key?"

Millicent laughed, then furrowed her brow. "Why would he be looking for a safe deposit key?" She stood up quickly, a hand to her mouth. "Oh no, oh no."

Tina and Jonie watched as Millicent ransacked her room. Millicent's eyes were watering, and she said, with a quivering voice, "He couldn't have known. Why would he? Oh no, oh no."

"So, you did have a safe deposit key in here?" Tina asked.

Millicent turned to her. "No one must ever find out what's in that safe deposit box. It's a matter of life and death! What are we going to do?"

Credits

Director... Theresa Erwin
Writers... Judy Flick
Jean Questel
Howard Simmons

Episode Fourteen

Regina woke, her body aching. Before she opened her eyes, she realized something wasn't right. Her head was throbbing, and her arms were stiff. There was something tight and rough binding her wrists together. She had trouble swallowing, because someone had stuffed a huge mass of fabric into her mouth as a gag.

She opened her eyes, immediately alert. She was tied up. *Think, Regina,* she commanded herself. But everything was so blurry. She remembered arriving at the hotel bar to meet the Count, who had never showed up! She had waited until finally she had to admit he wasn't going to arrive. She'd put the hotel key in her purse and left the bar to return to the lobby and see if she could get a refund for the room. She remembered walking along the side of the hotel, hearing footsteps gaining on her, and turning around only to feel something heavy hit her on the head.

She tried to move her arms, but they were tied too tightly behind her back. Her legs were also tied to the feet of the hotel room's chair; she couldn't even kick them out an inch. She tried to scream for help, but all that came out was a muffled moan.

Maybe if she could wriggle the chair to the corner of the desk, she could lift her arms up enough to use the desk's edge to saw through the rope! But as she tried to lift her body and leverage the chair to her left, she tipped dangerously. It was no use. If she fell, she was afraid she would seriously injure herself even further. Not to mention the even greater sense of helplessness she would feel when whoever did this to her returned.

As she racked her brain for some way out of this, she heard the sound of metal sliding into place. The click of a lock disengaged, and the door began to swing open. Into the room stepped someone she hadn't expected to see again... in this lifetime at least. A small figure with jet black hair and bangs. Someone who was supposed to be dead...

"Ah, I'm happy to see you're awake," said Chef Maxine, removing her sunglasses and hat. "I must be stronger than I thought to have knocked you out that long. Hopefully you're not concussed." Chef Maxine gave her a mocking expression of fake sympathy.

Regina tried to scream again and began frantically to wiggle her arms back and forth in a vain attempt to loosen the ropes binding her.

"Surprise!" Maxine said, laughing. "Oh, give it up, Regina. It's no use. Those are grade-A sailor knots. And even if you could scream through the gag, there's no one in this flea-ridden motel who would hear you or care. I would have expected the count to have better taste. But then, what would you expect him to spend on a side piece?"

Chef Maxine walked over to Regina and removed the gag. Regina breathed a sigh of relief then looked up, narrowing her eyes as she tried to see if there were any tell-tale signs that this person was not who they claimed to be. But it was Maxine, alright, right down to that big mole right beneath her left eye.

"Maxine, what on earth? Why am I tied up?"

"Oh, I think you know, Regina dear. You're going to be very, very sorry for all you've done."

"But you died! We saw them pull your head out of that soup pot. You were dead."

"Well," said Chef Maxine, "obviously you were wrong. I tried to get your attention before all of this got out of hand, but you ignored me. So now, you've left me no choice but to make an *executive* decision and eliminate you and the Count."

"No! Please, Maxine. It... it wasn't me. You have to know that I had nothing to do with it."

"I heard you didn't even shed a tear when they wheeled my body out, is that true?"

"No, of course not. I was so upset. We all were."

"And yet only a day later, you arrived here to meet up with a lover. And a resident! It's very unethical for someone who eventually wants to lead the state's Department of Senior Services. What would the governor say?"

"The Count is aware of my ambitions. And he's a consenting adult!"

"Oh, I bet he's consenting alright. Between you, his wife, and that pretty Millicent, he's got his hands full!" Maxine laughed. "Really, I'll be doing him a favor getting rid of you."

"No! I can help you. I know all the Count's secrets."

Maxine raised an eyebrow. "Really, like what?"

"Untie me and I'll tell you," Regina said. "The Count, he's working on something big..."

"Which is?"

"I... I'm not sure, he was going to tell me last night. If you let me go, I can talk to him and find out."

"You're lying. I know you and the Count are up to something," Maxine raged. "I don't need you to help me. No one needs you!"

And with that final proclamation, Maxine grabbed the gag that had been stuffed in Regina's mouth and unfurled it, revealing it to be her Shady Bluff apron. She grabbed both ends then wrapped the fabric around Regina's neck and began to tighten.

Maxine cackled as Regina turned blue. Regina tried to breathe, but it was no use. She looked up to see that the beauty mark under Maxine's eye was peeling off her face. Finally, unable to breath, her body gave up and everything went black.

Maxine stepped back and wiped sweat off her forehead. Regina's body would need to be disposed of, but she would need help with that. Luckily for her, Shady Bluff was full of people with terrible secrets they'd do anything to keep hidden.

Credits

Director... Sara Haugen
Writers... Maxi McGilton
Connie Perry
Howard Simmons

Episode Fifteen

The sound of the Count's soles on the floor echoed through the bank as he followed the manager to the security vault.

"I hope Ms. Trueworthy is doing okay. You understand that for her to send someone on her behalf is normally considered unorthodox, but, after the last visit, we could only sympathize, Mr. Trueworthy."

The Count tried to hide a smile as he was ushered in and both parties placed their keys into the safe deposit box. As long as you carried yourself with authority and acted as if you had every right to be doing what you were doing, no one ever dared question you, even when your lie was as blatant as being the husband to a woman who'd never remarried after her divorce.

The manager stepped back, but the Count dismissed him with a wave of his hand.

"Of course, sir. If you need anything or when you're done, simply press the buzzer here," the manager indicated a button on the table, "and I'll be right in."

Once the Count had the room to himself, he began to open the box. He couldn't believe that it was this easy! Millicent hadn't even known what was happening. Just a little drink, a little drug, and she had giggled the entire time he ransacked her apartment.

He ignored a small pang of regret. He had to admit she was gorgeous, and so sweet. And not always conniving like Regina and his wife. But it was better this way, even though she would never forgive his betrayal. Still, he wished that stupid Plant Operations Director had been able to find the key. The man was an idiot.

Count Dandy lifted the lid and frowned. The box was empty, save for a small envelope, the corner of which was lodged in the metal lip along the very back edge. He cursed and slammed his hand down on the buzzer.

Impatiently, he waited for the manager to let him out. He thought about opening the letter, but no, better to wait until he was back in the apartment where he could read it in absolute privacy.

As he entered the lobby of Shady Bluff Senior Living, his cellphone rang. The screen identified the number as Unlisted. Normally, the Count would never answer the phone from someone he didn't know. Too many leeches trying to scam people out of their money. But he was expecting this call.

"Hello?" he asked, waving his hand dismissively at the receptionist who was standing at her desk calling his name. She looked positively frantic, but he didn't have time for whatever she thought she needed to tell him.

"Is it taken care of?" said a voice on the other end.

"There's been a... how shall I put it... a hiccup."

"What do you mean?" The man's voice on the other end of the line was barely above a whisper, yet it communicated strength, authority, and above all, warning.

"The contents were not what we anticipated. Someone must have gotten there before me," said the Count. "But they did leave us something. It appears to be a note."

"A note?" the man said, and the Count noticed a small hesitation, a nervousness in the question. "What did it say?"

"Oh, a little of this, a little of that. It was most illuminating," lied the Count. He pressed the button to the elevator. The blasted thing was taking forever.

"I want you to destroy it," the man said. "And I want you to watch you do it. Set it on fire. Rip it into a thousand pieces and flush it down the toilet. But whatever you do, I want it on video so I can see it happen."

The Count smiled. "Of course, I'm sure you'd make it worth my while to eliminate something so valuable."

"Trust me, you will be taken care of."

"I hope you mean monetarily and that's not a threat, Senator," the Count said.

"I'm a man of my word, Count," said the Senator.

Count Dandy pursed his lips. The Senator's evasion of his question did not go unnoticed. He ended the phone call and pressed the button to the elevator again. He could feel his fury rising. The only thing stopping him from flying into a rage was the collateral he now carried with him: a note written, the Count assumed, by Millicent. And its contents held a secret to something the Senator was keen to see destroyed.

The Count knew he was in a very dangerous position, but he had been backed into a corner before and always fought his way out, emerging victorious and with those who would threaten him at his complete mercy.

He heard the sound of the elevator motor and the car descending from the floors above. He smiled to himself. No one was going to stop him from getting what he wanted.

Credits

Director... Pat Milsap
Writers... Kay Simpson
Marty Stater
Charlie Toplift
Howard Simmons

Episode Sixteen

"There's nothing else to talk about," the Countess said to Jimmy as he stared, flabbergasted, at the pistol she had pulled from her purse. She was perched on the edge of her husband's bed.

"You're threatening my mother," he said. His hands were squeezed into fists. He would do anything to protect his mom, including going back to jail.

The Countess smiled. "And you," she said. "Don't think that you can play the hero and make everything go away. If you were to go back to jail, your mom's role in hiding you would come to light. And she would go to jail. If you tell anyone about what I'm up to, I'll expose you... and you and your mom will go to jail. If something happens to me, a *friend* will expose you... and you and your mom will go to jail. You might not mind being behind bars, but I bet Regina Inkler wouldn't last very long."

"So, what happens next, huh? You just keep me under your thumb for the rest of my life?" Jimmy asked, a note of desperation coming to the surface.

"No, Jimmy, just until we can see our plan through to the end. I just need to make sure you don't get cold feet."

Jimmy gritted his teeth and tried to think. But thinking came hard for Jimmy sometimes and he grunted in frustration.

The Countess stood up, the pistol safely tucked away in her purse again. "I'm not going to sit here all day and wait for my husband to show up. Lord knows what he and your mother have been up to. Can't even bother to show up for work from what I hear."

Jimmy frowned. In all of the commotion earlier he'd not noticed his mother wasn't in the building. It wasn't like her at all to be late for work.

"I'll leave and you can sneak out a few moments after me. Take the stairs, I don't want anyone to see us together," the Countess said. And she opened the door, walking quickly to the elevator.

As Jimmy started to leave, he heard a sound come from the closet. He stopped and looked back. But before he could investigate, he heard the elevator ding as it opened for Countess Lily, reminding him that a resident or caregiver could come down the hall at any moment and there would be no plausible reason for him to be in the Count's room. He pulled the door behind him as he left.

Cordelia, having banged her calf against something in the closet, sighed with relief when she heard the door close for the second time. She had been certain she was about to be discovered, and, considering the two parties on the other side of the door, she didn't like her chances of getting away unscathed.

As she stepped out of the closet, she looked around to make sure no one was waiting to ambush her. But the room was empty. She turned back to the closet, staring at its contents.

Inside were rows of small screens, all of them broadcasting the apartments of Shady Bluff residents. Even Cordelia's room was under surveillance. Beyond the invasion of privacy, the embarrassment of her private moments and acts recorded for another to watch, Cordelia was uncertain what the Count could possibly gain by keeping his neighbors under surveillance.

As she scanned the screens one final time, she saw in one of the displays Millicent, Tina and Jonie sitting around a small table. Cordelia immediately recognized it as Millicent's room.

Cordelia crept out of the Count's apartment, forgetting to close the closet door where she'd been hiding.

As she left, she smoothed her hair back and walked quickly to Millicent's apartment. Hard feelings be darned, she had to warn her that the Count was up to something that involved her and put her in harm's way.

When Millicent opened the door, Cordelia braced herself to be rebuffed. But instead, Millicent, with eyes puffy from tears, smiled with obvious relief.

"Thank God you're here, Cordelia. Something terrible has happened. I don't know what to do," Millicent said.

"I have bad news of my own, I'm afraid," said Cordelia. She took a seat at the table and the friends, putting misunderstandings behind them, told each other of what they had learned.

Credits

Director... Leah Gallas
Writers... Virginia Bailey
Debbie Dewey
Judy Silcox
Howard Simmons

Episode Seventeen

The Countess had a bad habit of talking to herself. As she rode the elevator down, she huffed, "I have a feeling my husband is somewhere in this building. I've just not caught that snake yet."

She checked her nails to ensure they'd not chipped. She cleared her throat. The elevator jerked as it came to a halt, causing her to lose her balance a little. Ruffled, she tried to compose herself as the doors opened... to reveal her husband, Count Dandy Caruthers, standing in front of her, his mouth hanging open in surprise.

"Just what do you think you are doing?" asked the Countess, who wanted to scream, but managed to keep her voice to a hiss.

"My dear wife, I am delighted to see you," the Count said, smiling unctuously. He made to take his wife's hand, but she pulled it away.

"If you think I don't know what you've been doing, you're sorely mistaken, *Husband,*" she replied. "I know what you've been up to and with whom you've been up to it."

"Don't be absurd, Lily. Have you taken your pills today? You know how you can get a little confused if you forget them."

"One day I'll have your head on a plate, Dandy, mark my words."

"The day you try that, sweet one, is the day you'll find yourself six feet underground."

The Countess smiled, a cold, calculating smile that instantly set the Count's palms to sweating. "Where's your darling? The woman who runs this place? Regina Inkler, I believe her name is?"

"How would I know?"

"Don't play dumb with me, Dandy. Like I said, I know what you've been up to."

"I assume she took the day off. I don't know or care what the administrator of this building does."

"I wonder," the Countess said, "if you would change your tune if something were to happen to her."

The Count's face reddened, and he took a step toward her, hands outstretched as if to throttle her. But the Countess was quicker and lighter on her feet, and she dodged, one leg thrust out so the Count tripped. His head slammed against the elevator's metal door.

The Countess looked down. "What a pathetic excuse for a husband," she said. She lifted her skirt and stepped over his body.

As she made her way out, she signaled to a caregiver leaving an apartment. "I believe you might want to check on the Count," said the Countess. "It seems he fainted. He might have a concussion."

And she walked on, her heels clanking against the tile floor.

Back at Downing Dumpf's Motel, Patrick, the motel's part-time and only housekeeper and maintenance man, who was finally getting around to painting over the graffiti on one of the walls, had watched the woman in a chef's jacket speed away.

There was something about her movements that had the hairs on the back of Patrick's neck standing up. *There can't be a lick of good in this,* he thought as he glanced toward the room she'd recently exited.

Patrick had been employed by the motel long enough to know that sometimes bad things happened in these rooms. No one took a room at this motel for the pleasure of it. It was quiet, hidden, and everyone was willing to look the other way when something happened. The owner had told Patrick that he was to mind his own business. "The less we know, the less trouble we can get in," he'd said to Patrick.

But Patrick ignored that memory, his curiosity getting the better of him. He set the paintbrush down and dashed to the room. The door was locked, a Do Not Disturb sign hanging from the handle.

He unlocked the door and stepped inside, taking in an overturned table and a chair with more rope than anyone should need in a hotel puddled around its legs. "Oh my gosh, what's happened here?" Patrick said aloud.

He took a step closer to the chair and saw, glinting on the floor, a gold bracelet. From any other angle he would have missed it as it was mostly under the bed, hidden from sight. Patrick thought, *If I look the other way, they probably will too. And I don't get paid enough anyway. I deserve a little bonus.*

He bent down to pick up the jewelry, but as he pulled it, he realized it was attached to something. He gave a tug, and the bracelet gave way, as did an arm, its hand fastened in a grip.

Uh-oh, thought Patrick, springing back quickly. He didn't want anything to do with a dead body. Nevertheless, he knelt, going to all fours to get a better look at what had been pushed beneath the bed.

I better get out of here, he thought. But just as he was about to rise again, he heard a wheezing sound followed by a shallow inhalation. The woman was alive!

Patrick almost wished that she wasn't, because now he had only one option and it would probably get him fired. He pulled his cell phone from his pocket and dialed 911.

The Countess pulled into the parking lot of a convenience store, driving around to the back, where a lone car sat idling. She crept up toward it until her window was parallel with the other driver's. Simultaneously, the windows were lowered and the Countess smiled at the car's occupant.

"Do you know how long I've been waiting?" the woman in the chef's jacket said.

The Countess's smile cooled. She did not like being addressed in this manner. But she decided to overlook it. She didn't have time to put this woman in her place. "Is it done?" the Countess asked.

"Of course," the woman spat. "If I can drown my own sister in a vat of soup, I can take care of some nobody in over her head."

"I'm glad to hear it. Your mole, by the way, is falling off."

The woman glanced in the rearview mirror and pulled the little brown spot off. "Cheap costume effects," the woman laughed. "To think, the only thing keeping me and my twin from being identical was an ugly mole. Poor Maxine, I hoped they were able to cover it when they prepared her for burial."

The Countess frowned. This woman was heartless. Useful, but heartless. Then again, what could you expect from someone's evil twin? "I'll follow you, Minnie," she said.

And Minnie made her way back to the highway, the Countess trailing close behind.

Credits

Director... Emma Wray
Writers... Ann Catlow
Howard Simmons

Episode Eighteen

Jimmy clomped down the stairs, scratching his chin as he tried to think of a way out of the mess he'd gotten himself in. Lost in thought, he didn't see the other person heading up the stairs, also with her head down.

They collided, "Ahhh!" screamed Pippi as she felt herself tumbling back. Before she could fall, though, Jimmy grabbed her wrist and pulled her toward him.

Pippi, leaning against him, rubbed her head. "You saved my life," she said. "I should have been looking where I was going."

"It's my fault! I wasn't paying attention," Jimmy said.

Pippi smiled and looked up at him. "Penny for your thoughts?"

"Oh, I dunno," Jimmy said. He might not be the sharpest box in the crayon, but he knew the less you told people, the less they could use your words against you.

"Well, I can tell you that I was lost in thought, too. And it was about something very strange." Pippi looked at him, considering. Why not ask Jimmy his opinion on what Mal had shown her? He was often in the background of Shady Bluff. Perhaps he'd seen or heard something!

"Jimmy, do you know why the tulips in the garden were burned?" she asked.

"No, why were they?" Jimmy responded.

"No, I'm asking you if *you* know anything about them."

Jimmy shook his head. "I was surprised to see someone do that. As much work as Cordelia put into that flower bed, it was as if someone was doing it just to hurt her."

Pippi thought again about her discovery of the tulips. Her first response had been to get Cordelia to show her. But what had made her go out to the garden in the first place? She frowned, trying to remember. She had been on her way to the supply closet to get out games for board game night and she saw Mal coming toward her... "I think Millicent is smoking in the garden again," Mal had said. "Someone's gonna need to clean up the cigarette butts."

Which of course meant that Pippi was going to need to do it, because Mal never helped with things like that. It was a not-so-well-kept secret that Millicent Trueworthy snuck cigarettes, but no one wanted to get her into trouble by telling the executive director.

But when Pippi went out to the garden, there hadn't been any cigarette butts. Just the scorched area where Cordelia's flowers had been burned.

Pippi looked up at Jimmy. "I think someone is trying to frame Cordelia." And she began to tell Jimmy about the notes Mal had received since her husband's car crash.

Jimmy agreed that it didn't sound like something Cordelia Buttons would do. "Maybe we should go talk to her?"

Pippi agreed, feeling confident that she and Jimmy together would be able to glean a clue from the notes Mal had shown her.

But when they drew near to the Wellness Director's office, they found she was already with someone. Luckily, they only had to wait another few minutes before the director's door opened and Mal walked with the Count out to the hall. Count Dandy bowed his head in Pippi's direction and then walked away, rubbing the back of his head.

Mal smiled at Pippi and Jimmy. "What brings you two to see me?"

"I want to see those letters, Ms. Practiss," Jimmy said, as they followed Mal into the office. Pippi closed the door so no one would hear.

"Pippi, I told you that in confidence," Mal said. She moved behind her desk, trying to control her annoyance.

Pippi smiled. "Which is why I told Jimmy. He is very smart and a good listener. I'm confident in him, too! We can help."

Jimmy blushed at the compliments. "*Can* I see the letters, Ms. Practiss?"

"No, you may not!" Mal said. "I don't mean to be rude, but those letters were shown to Pippi, and I assumed she would keep them private and not tell anyone."

"I'm sorry, Jimmy. I feel so stupid," Pippi said after Mal threw them out of her office. "But I just don't understand why Mal would think Cordelia was sending her threatening letters. Ms. Buttons wouldn't hurt a fly!"

"Maybe," Jimmy said, "Mal *wants* you to think Cordelia sent them."

"But why?"

"I don't know," Jimmy said, stroking his jaw. "But if I've learned anything since my time in the slam– , er, the world, it's that everyone's got a secret reason for doing anything. You can't trust anyone, Pippi."

"Not even you?" she asked, her eyes twinkling in hope as she looked up at Jimmy.

"Least of all me, Pippi."

"Oh, Jimmy. I'm so afraid something bad is going on!"

And Jimmy wrapped his arms around Pippi for a brief moment. Then he pulled away. "I guess I better get back to work."

Pippi smiled. "Okay, but keep an ear and an eye out, alright?"

As Mal took a deep breath in her office, she could feel herself starting to shake. When she had found the Count in the hallway in front of the elevator, he'd been knocked out cold. How relieved she was to hear him snort right before he woke up. "That evil wife will be the death of me," he had said as he sat up. Despite his assurances he was fine, she insisted he come back to her office so she could look him over.

But despite her alarm at his possible concussion, it was not any potential injury that had frightened her. For as he stood, a small, folded piece of paper fell from his jacket pocket. Mal instantly recognized it: it was the same cornflower color as those ominous notes she'd received. Before the Count could notice it was missing, she snatched it up and put it in her pocket.

She focused on encouraging the Count to talk. She asked him if he felt nauseous, checked that his vision wasn't blurry, feigned interest as he recounted his wife's violence toward him.

But she could only think about the letter she had taken, and with every moment felt more and more desperate and afraid that he was going to realize it was missing.

Now that she had gotten rid of Pippi and that himbo Jimmy, Mal opened the letter that had fallen out of the Count's pocket.

But the contents were something completely different than she expected. It was a confession of sorts, of lost love, secrets and betrayal. Mal read every page, her eyes widening with every new paragraph...

Credits

Director... Coby Roark
Writers... Gail Thurman
Howard Simmons

Episode Nineteen

As Herman sat in his office, going through all the employee paperwork he had to complete, his mind wandered to the conversation he'd just had with Percival. He winced at the recollection that he'd unburdened himself to a resident, confessing to his affair with Chef Maxine and her warnings about Regina and Millicent: that Regina wasn't to be trusted and Millicent was likely in trouble.

He knew he was missing several pieces of a very large puzzle. He shook the thoughts from his head and returned his attention to the computer. But just as he began to get back into the flow of the endless paperwork, the receptionist, Rebecca, popped her head in. "There's a call holding. It's Millicent's daughter."

Oh boy, thought Herman. *Yet another person from my complicated past.* He picked up the handset and brought it to his ear, pressing the button for the correct extension where the caller was parked.

"Good morning, Jessica. This is Herman."

"Good morning, Herman. Is the Executive Director not in today?"

Herman paused. No one knew where Regina was. He'd texted and called her cell phone, but not received an answer.

"She took the morning off," he said. He tried not to feel wounded that Jessica had not wanted to speak to him, but, considering their history, it wasn't really a surprise.

"Okay, you would think the receptionist would know that," Jessica said. "I'm calling about my mom."

"I assumed as much. What's going on?"

"Have you noticed anything going on with her? Is she doing okay?"

"She seems to be fine, from what I've seen and heard," Herman said.

"I'm a little concerned. You know Mom and I Zoom at least a couple times a week, but she missed our scheduled time, and, when I finally got a hold of her, she seemed paranoid and skittish. She's always loved to fill me in on the community's gossip, but she didn't want to tell me about anything going on. She actually said that, Herman, 'I can't tell you about anything going on.' Doesn't that seem strange?"

Herman admitted that it was a little weird, but he also thought that a reluctance to gossip one time didn't mean that Millicent was paranoid. Not that he said this to Jessica. She knew her mother better than he did, and Herman hadn't been out of his office much lately. What with all his paperwork he had to do.

But he wanted to make Jessica happy. She'd been a teacher to his two daughters when they were freshmen in high school. They'd met at the first parent teacher conference of that school year. He talked to her regularly about his daughters' education, and then, as he got to know her, began to reach out more and more often. Herman knew he was charming, and he was certain that he could win Jessica's heart, too. He was a good dad, he was fun to talk to, and he knew he was a handsome man.

But Jessica rejected him. Again and again, she said no to his offers of coffee, dinner, an extra meeting after school hours to talk about the girls' performance. Eventually, he realized that, even though Jessica would look at him with those large, brown eyes and he knew she wanted to say yes, she was too professional and self-possessed, and driven by an inner moral compass that he could not understand.

As his attempts became more desperate, calling her home, sending her flowers, he found it hard to meet his wife's gaze. He knew that at any moment he could be caught trying to woo his daughters' teacher. And his wife, Bonnie, had already told him that if he didn't get his 'extra-curricular' activities under control, she would leave him and take the girls.

So, he gave up his pursuit, cut the possibility of seeing Jessica out of his life completely. He found a house in another school district. And it was the kind of home that Bonnie always wanted: a four-bedroom Georgian that looked out on a quiet street. If Bonnie ever suspected the real reason why they moved, she never mentioned it. And Herman had kept his wandering eye focused on his family and his home.

Until Maxine, came along, of course, and wrecked everything.

"Herman?" Jessica said on the call, interrupting his train of thought.

"Hmm? Yes?"

"I asked when Regina was going to be back. I think I should talk to her. You said she took the morning off?"

"The morning or the day, I forget which. You know, I'm always so inundated with paperwork I sometimes lose track of things."

"I thought you monitored everyone's time off?"

Oh, right, Herman thought. I did tell her that, the day she moved Millicent in. That was a surprise, to find Jessica in the lobby holding her mother's hand as they looked around the foyer. His heart had jumped into his throat at the sight of her. She was so beautiful.

"Well, I do, but Regina is a special case, of course. I can't demand that my boss give me her whereabouts at all times."

"That's no way for anyone to run a community," Jessica said. She was quickly shedding her sweet side. Herman found he had a lump in his throat. She could be so *forceful* when she needed to be. He found it very attractive.

"I'll check in on your mom, Jessica," Herman said. "I'll be in touch soon."

Jessica, Maxine, Regina... how did he always get so mixed up in everything? He was in love with Regina, but hearing Jessica's voice... It made him want to do whatever he could for her.

He stood up and went to find Millicent Trueworthy and see if she was feeling poorly or if there was anything worrying her. He did recall a conversation Millicent and Regina had had the week before. Millicent had been upset, but while he repeatedly heard the words "community" and "gossip," he'd not thought much of it. But he did remember Regina being awfully worked up after Millicent left her office.

And it was pretty strange that Millicent would even be sharing gossip with Regina. They weren't friends and Herman knew Regina to be very good about setting professional boundaries: she had told him they couldn't start dating until after she'd been promoted to a regional director.

He squared his shoulders. He was next in charge if Regina was out of commission and, until he heard from her, he would take command. He mentally went over all that he had to do today: finish payroll, MC the pickleball classic at noon, help Pippi with the preparations for the Alzheimer's donation booth this afternoon...

But the first thing he needed to do, before he got back to all that paperwork, was talk to Millicent.

Credits

Director... Katarina Vrhovac
Writers... Larry Beans
Joe Difiore
Bob Jokela
Howard Simmons

Episode Twenty

Cordelia, Millicent, Tina, and Jonie sat around Millicent's table in her apartment. Each of them leaned over their cups of tea with an expression of intense focus as they mulled over what had been shared.

"Okay, I think the first thing we should do is go over once more what we know: The Count moved in on Tuesday. The next morning, Chef Brûlée was murdered. That same day, I found a letter in what was once my tulip bed that someone, we don't know who, had until midnight Friday – *that's tonight* – or else. But we don't know what they had to do by tonight.

"Millicent, the Count asked you out Wednesday and when you got home, the apartment had been ransacked. He then came back the next day, this would have been yesterday, and gave you several drinks that we suspect he spiked with a hallucinogenic drug so that he could continue to look for the safe deposit key to your bank, which we also assume he found and probably used this morning. While the Count was out, I found that he's been monitoring all of us. We don't know for what purposes or how he got all of those cameras installed, but I think I have a good idea about that last point…"

As Cordelia was recounting all they shared, there came a knock on the door. It was Mal, the Wellness Director.

"I'm sorry to bother you, Millicent, but I had to come by. I found something that belongs to you." And Mal held out the letter that the Count had dropped outside the elevator.

"You better come in, Mal," said Millicent, stepping back. When Mal saw the other women at the table, she hesitated, her eyes lingering on Cordelia, whom she still believed responsible for sending her threating letters regarding her husband's death.

Mal had overcome a lot of trials in her life. Better to confront one's problems head on, she believed.

"Before we go any further, I have to ask a question of Cordelia." Mal faced Cordelia and took a deep breath. "Why are you sending me letters and riddles about my husband's death, Cordelia?"

Everyone gasped, all eyes turning to Cordelia. "What are you talking about?" Cordelia asked.

As Mal explained the letters, Cordelia shook her head. "I haven't been sending you letters, Mal. I swear. But I did find a letter that night you helped me in the garden." And Cordelia once again explained what happened and the note's contents.

"If that letter was meant for you, Mal, then it means someone is expecting something from you by midnight tonight. Do you know who?" Tina asked.

"They could be referring to me cashing my life insurance check, that seems to be the letters' main focus: getting me to accept that million-dollar payout," Mal said. "But I can't do it. I know it might seem crazy, but some part of me feels like Randy could still be alive. I feel like cashing that check means giving up hope on my husband."

Millicent began to pace back and forth. She was clasping her hands together tightly, her mouth set in a grim line.

"Millicent," said Tina. "I think you have something to tell them."

Millicent turned around, tears shimmering in her eyes.

"No, I don't."

Cordelia could tell that Millicent was holding something back, but she knew better than to push. "I think we should read that letter Mal found."

Millicent took a deep breath and handed it over to Cordelia. "This was something I never wanted anyone to know while I was alive. But if it was found, it means that everything else in that safe deposit box was also discovered and the Count knows all my secrets now."

Cordelia began to read. "Millicent, is this true?"

Millicent nodded and Cordelia went to her friend and embraced her.

"What does it say?" asked Tina, somewhat impatiently.

"When I was a young woman, I worked as a volunteer for a local politician who was running for the State Senate," said Millicent. "He was only a few years older, and so handsome and charismatic. You could tell he was going places. Well, one thing led to another, and we started seeing each other. Secretly. He was white and you know how folks were back then, a white politician with a black girlfriend?"

Millicent looked at Tina and Jonie who were nodding their heads in understanding.

"We knew it couldn't last, but we were in love, or so I thought. It would have run its course, I'm sure, and we would have gone our separate ways after he moved to the capitol. But then I got pregnant.

"And suddenly it was as if I'd tried to trap him. He couldn't get away from me fast enough. I was so embarrassed and ashamed that I kept it to myself.

Only he and I knew about it. He was elected and by then I was beginning to show. He paid for me to take a 'long vacation' so that I could have the baby away from prying eyes and questions. 'For the sake of your reputation,' he told me.

"I gave birth alone in a hospital several states away. The baby only lived a few hours before it passed away. Or that was what I told him. I think some small, silly part of me thought that he would take me back. I gave the baby up for adoption and returned home to find him in the State Senate, dating the Governor's pretty blonde daughter. A few years later he ran and won a seat in the U.S. Senate, where he's been for decades now.

"Is it? Was it... Senator Golden?" asked Tina. Millicent nodded.

"But he's running for President in the next election!" said Jonie.

"There's more to the story," said Millicent, "because eventually our paths crossed again. I know some things about the Senator that he wouldn't like getting out to the press. I'm not proud of it, but I used that knowledge to help my children's education."

"Is that what was in the safe deposit box? Evidence that could be used against the Senator?" asked Cordelia.

"Yep, and if it's in the Count's hands, then I'm in danger," said Millicent.

The group was silent, mulling over this news when Mal spoke up. "But I don't understand how that pertains to me or the notes I've been getting."

"I think I may know, although it's purely speculation at this point," said Cordelia. "Millicent, did you keep track of your child after it was adopted?"

"Him. I had a boy. I named him Randall, although his adopted parents shortened it... to Randy."

Mal cried out in surprise. "Do you mean? Are you saying?"

Tina spoke up. "Mal was married to your son, Millicent?"

Millicent began to cry. "Yes, it's true. I couldn't say anything because I was afraid of what the Senator would do if he knew his son was alive. You don't know how many times I wanted to tell you, Mal. How my heart grieved with you when he had that accident."

"But you kept it a secret," Mal said. "Randy always wondered about his birth parents. It was the one thing he said he regretted, that he never got to meet them, to ask them about his biological family and why they chose to give him up."

Millicent reached out a hand to comfort Mal, but Mal stepped away, her face a mask of hurt. "I don't know what to say, Millicent. I remember how you two talked during your first Christmas party here, just months before his accident. 'What a lovely lady,' he said. 'She acted so interested in everything I had to say.' This whole time you could have told the truth. You could have given him that, but you chose to pretend he was a stranger."

Before Millicent could respond, Mal turned and left the apartment.

Millicent sat on the bed, her head in her hands. Jonie went to her and wrapped her arm around Millicent's shoulder.

"We still don't know what's going to happen tonight," said Cordelia. "And we only have a few hours left to figure it out. Some of our lives may depend on it!"

Credits

Director... Pat Milsap
Writers... Kay Simpson
Marty Stater
Charlie Toplift
Howard Simmons

Season Finale, Part One:
Episode Twenty-One

As Cordelia unlocked her apartment door and stepped inside, her focus was completely on the mysteries at Shady Bluff. *What was going to happen at midnight? Why was the Count spying on the residents? Did the Count kill Chef Maxine?*

She turned on the light and gasped. There was someone waiting for her in her room. The figure, who had been sitting on her cedar hope chest at the end of the bed, stood up.

"Hello, Cordelia," said Phillip Hedd, the community's Maintenance Director. He was an inch shy of six feet and much taller than Cordelia. He raked a hand across his buzzcut, his pink scalp showing through the shorn gray and white hair.

Cordelia squared her shoulders back. "What are you doing in my room, Phillip? You're supposed to give me 24 hours' notice. Unless it's an emergency."

Phillip smiled and shrugged. "Guess I thought it couldn't wait."

"What do you want?" Cordelia asked. She had always been uncomfortable around him. Most residents thought him pleasant enough with his good ole boy charm, but she saw through it.

"I don't know why you're so upset," he said. "Seems like we're both used to going into places we shouldn't." He grimaced. "Sometimes it can get us into trouble. So, I thought I would come by and see what you'd been up to before I go to the Executive Director and report you for breaking and entering. I don't remember hearing that you and the Count had become friends. So, tell me why you would be in his room when I know that he wasn't in his apartment?"

Cordelia felt her hands go sweaty. She was certain that no one had seen her come out. The hallway had been clear. But then she realized and cursed herself for being so stupid. There were cameras everywhere! And she already knew that it must have been Phillip who had set them up for the Count inside every resident's apartment.

"I don't think you'll be doing that," Cordelia said, trying to sound more confident than she felt.

"And why is that?" Mr. Hedd stepped closer.

"Because I doubt Ms. Inkler knows that you and her newest tenant have been spying on all the residents. She probably wouldn't be very happy to hear that you were betraying our right to privacy, would she?"

The Maintenance Director smiled, but this time all false kindness was gone from it. "That's where you'd be wrong, Cordelia. But something tells me you won't ever get the chance to tell her."

And before Cordelia could try to get away, he was on her. Grabbing her by the shoulders, he spun her around and threw her into her bookcase. She didn't even have a chance to scream.

Percival was nervous. He was set to play in the first pickleball match of the tournament today. He could feel his stomach roiling in ways that didn't inspire much confidence in his chances. He'd been captain of the police force's softball team "back in the day," as he liked to call it when reminiscing, and despite the extra 30 or, let's face it, 50 pounds he'd gained since his time on the job, he still thought of himself as in shape.

But he knew everyone was going to be watching the games, and, while Roland Niemeyer was the perfect partner and their chances were good, the idea that Cordelia would be watching made him want to forfeit and hide in his room. He couldn't stand the very thought that he might goof up, or God forbid, fall in front of her. His pride wouldn't take it. He knew that he and Cordelia were destined to fall in love, but he just couldn't seem to get on the right footing with her.

But he also couldn't bail on Roland. That wouldn't look good either. And Percival had never backed down from a fight of any kind. He took a deep breath as he strode down the hall, swinging his arms wide, rotating his wrists, and almost knocked Sara Lakshmi's head off.

"Watch it, Percy!" she called as she backed away. Sara, who lived a few doors down from Percival with her husband, had a way of scowling and laughing at the same time and Percy smiled at her sheepishly.

"Sorry, Sara!" he said.

"Don't make me sorry I put money down on you and Roland taking the top spot."

Percival was flattered. "I'll try my best," he said, suddenly feeling lighter from her confidence in him.

"And don't tell Rakesh. He's still angry at me for losing at the blackjack table last month."

Percival nodded. Rakesh Lakshmi was the exact opposite of his wife. Where Sara was opinionated, quick to laughter and anger, and was a risk-taker by nature, Rakesh was quiet and reserved. Percival liked them very much and would sometimes daydream about him and Cordelia double dating with them.

When he got to the pickleball court, he walked over to his partner, who was alternating jumping jacks with pushups. "Gee, Roland, save some energy for the court," Percival said.

Roland sprang up and slapped his partner on the arm. "Gotta get the blood pumping, Percy! Limber up the joints. Join in, I only have 50 jumping jacks to go."

"Um, no thanks," Percival said. "I think I'll just do some stretches." He scanned the gathering crowd for Cordelia. But neither she nor any of her friends were around. He checked his watch: 11:45 am.

Herman had been on his way to talk to Millicent about her daughter's concerns. But before he made it to her room, his cell phone rang. It was the front desk. "Yes?" he replied as he brought the phone to his ear. The receptionist, Rebecca, was breathlessly telling him that the *police* were on the line. "Go ahead and transfer them," he said.

After a brief pause, the line connected and Herman said, "This is Herman Usurpera."

"Mr. Usurpera, this is Lieutenant Danvers. I'm sorry to interrupt your morning, but I was needing to speak with you about one of your coworkers, Regina Inkler."

"Regina? Is she okay?"

There was a momentary pause and Herman felt his knees go weak. Something had happened to Regina.

"I'm afraid to tell you that Ms. Inkler has been the victim of an attack. She's currently in the hospital."

"Is she okay? Did she ask you to call me?" Herman imagined Regina whispering his name as she was wheeled into the hospital, finally recognizing in her moment of need that he was the one who truly loved her and would take care of her.

"I'm afraid not," Lt. Danvers said. "Ms. Inkler is in a coma. We had no way to identify her next of kin. We were unable to unlock her cell phone, but we found her business card in her purse. Right now, Mr.

Usurpera, you're the only person who seems to give a damn about the poor woman. She's lucky to be alive."

The tournament was not off to a great start. Herman was supposed to MC, but, after a few minutes past the official start time, Pippi had run out of the building. Wild-eyed, her face as red as her hair from sprinting, she came to a sudden halt in front of Mal, who was serving as a judge. Percival was close enough to hear Pippi tell the Wellness Director that Regina was in the hospital and that Herman had left to go be with her. They conferred for a few moments and decided that the tournament should go on.

Percival and Roland took their spots on their end of the court. Roland was the first to serve and his aim was always perfect. The crowd applauded as they scored their first point.

Such an easy start to the game should have put Percival's mind at ease, but instead it allowed it to wander to what Pippi and Mal had been saying. Pippi didn't know what had happened, only that Regina had been seriously injured and was in the hospital. Herman hadn't said more before he bolted for his car. But the receptionist had told Pippi it was the police who called.

It could have been an accident, but Percival knew it wasn't. There were too many strange things going on. He wondered if what happened to Regina could somehow be connected to Chef Maxine's murder.

The ball sailed past him, and he heard the crowd groan while his opponents high fived. "Hey, Percy. Wake up!" Roland said.

"Sorry." Percival shook his head and tried to focus on the next serve. Luckily, it landed in the area of their side of the court called the kitchen, allowing Percival to jog up and underhand it back over the net.

As the ball made its way back and forth, Percival found himself getting into the rhythm of the game. He wondered if Cordelia was watching. He hoped she would be impressed.

He quickly checked the crowd. Millicent, Tina and Jonie were clustered together watching the match. All of them seemed slightly distracted. Cordelia wasn't with them. That was odd. It wasn't like Cordelia to be far from her best friends.

If both sides were evenly matched, the game could take 50 minutes, but, as it was, Roland and Percival bested their opponents rather quickly: in just under a half hour they'd won 11-6.

After shaking hands with the other team, Percival walked back to the building. He had time before their next match, and he wanted to check in on Cordelia. He had a terrible feeling.

The elevator dinged its arrival to the ground floor and Percival stepped back to let the Maintenance Director off. He was carrying a large cedar chest on a dolly.

"Looks like you got your hands full," Percival said.

"Oh yeah, yeah." Phillip said, looking both ways down the hall. He looked nervous.

"Where you heading with that? Need a hand?" Percival reached to steady the chest, which was cinched closed with nylon straps.

"NO!" Phillip said and Percival paused, perplexed.

"Everything okay?"

"It's just heavy and I don't want to trouble you with it. Plus, if something happened." Phillip gave a rattled laugh. "Don't wanna get sued."

"I wouldn't do that, Phillip," said Percival.

"Oh, I know. I know. But still. Gotta follow the rules, haha."

"Alright, well I was just on my way to visit Cordelia. You see her? She didn't come to the game."

"Cordelia? No, no why would you ask that?"

What is going on with this guy? Percival wondered. "Isn't that her chest? I recognize the doves carved on the top. It was her hope chest from her mother when she was a teenager."

"Right, right." Phillip said, and he was now looking a very sick shade of green. "But she wasn't there when I got it. She'd asked me to put it into storage for her. But we don't have room here, so I offered to put it into the community's storage place in town."

"Oh, I see. Well, you be careful. You look a little sick. Don't strain yourself."

"I won't, I won't," Phillip said, then laughed that strange, forced laugh again.

Percival watched the Maintenance Director make his way to the exit down the hall. Phillip glanced back as he maneuvered out the door. He looked annoyed that he was being watched. Percival nodded as a goodbye gesture then stepped onto the elevator.

Credits

Director... Caitlyn Pec
Writers... Connie Capps
Howard Simmons

Season Finale, Part Two:
Episode Twenty-Two

As Phillip drove the truck, he worked out what he should do. Once they realized that Cordelia was missing, it would only be a little while before Percival mentioned seeing him with the hope chest. And then they would want to see it. And what was inside it. And Phillip would be in a lot of trouble if they saw that.

He racked his brain for choices. He couldn't store it inside his house, he couldn't take it to the storage shed. He'd have to bury it. He had a backhoe on his property, so it would be easy work. He could just dig a hole in his backyard, bury her... *it*, he corrected himself. Best not to think about what had happened. He did what he was told and that was all there was to it. And after the chest was under several feet of dirt, he could plant some flowers or something. Tulips, maybe. That would be ironic, seeing as how he'd burned Cordelia's tulips. When he'd set fire to the tulips, he thought it had been a good way to warn her. Keep her from getting curious like she always did, but it apparently had backfired, making her even more nosy than she normally was.

"Curiosity killed the cat," he said out loud, but didn't find it funny. *Cats have nine lives,* he thought, and shivered.

Millicent and Tina were in the lobby, setting up the Alzheimer's donation table for when the tournament after-party began. Cordelia was supposed to be leading the fundraising effort, but she hadn't answered her phone or the door when the two had stopped by to see why she wasn't picking up.

It didn't feel right, but Millicent and Tina had their to-do list and there was too much going on to get distracted. Before Cordelia, Tina, and Jonie had left Millicent's apartment that morning, they'd all agreed to go about as if nothing were different today. But they were all keeping an eye and an ear out for anything out of the ordinary. "If it seems fishy, let us know," Cordelia had said.

And now Cordelia was nowhere to be found.

They put out a tablet to take donations by credit and debit card, a jar for cash donations, and placed bags beneath the table in case someone wanted to donate items to be sold at the next fundraiser auction.

As they set up, they saw a car pull up to the entrance. It was a sleek, red Tesla. Millicent watched the driver, a short, stout man carrying a medical bag close to his body enter and approach the front desk. The gentleman had a white Van Dyke beard and mustache and was wearing a three-piece pinwale navy-blue suit. A red tie stood out from his crisp white shirt. Millicent thought he looked like a cross between Colonel Sanders and the villain Draco in her favorite Bond film, *On Her Majesty's Secret Service.*

The man was speaking in low tones with the receptionist. He handed her a card. While his face was calm, his speech neutral (and too low for Millicent to hear), his words were causing the young woman to become paler and paler. Once the man stopped speaking, she nodded, stood up, then opened the door to Regina's office. She then sat down at her desk, picked up the phone's receiver and began speaking to someone.

In a few moments, Mal appeared, her face flushed. She looked, Millicent thought, a little frightened.

"I'd give anything to hear that conversation," Millicent said.

Mal entered Regina's office to find the small, yet imposing man seated behind Regina's desk. "Can I help you?" she asked.

"Yes, my dear, you can. Take a seat." He gestured at the chair in front of the desk. Mal obeyed. He leaned across the desk, offering her a business card, which she took and read aloud.

"Basil Q. Forthright, M.D. Medical Director for Cagnotte Senior Living."

"Yes, that's right. As you probably know, Cagnotte owns Shady Bluff Senior Living. They've sent me here to, for lack of a better way of putting it, *clean up your mess*. I'm to take on oversight immediately. But I understand your Executive Director and Human Resources Director are both out of the office?"

Mal nodded. "Regina, that's our Executive Director, she's in a coma. Herman went to visit her."

"Why on earth would he do that? She's in a coma, what does he think he can do?"

Mal didn't reply. He continued, "All the better, I suppose. If the ED is taking a break from running the community, she will have no objection to me setting up my office here."

"But... but... this is our director's office," stuttered Mal.

"All the better," Dr. Forthright exclaimed. "There is plenty of room for my diplomas."

Dr. Forthright pressed the button for the receptionist on the phone and leaned toward the speaker. "Please have someone get my diplomas out of my Tesla. I'm assuming your Maintenance Director can take care of it.

"Now, I will begin examining the residents immediately for my files. I can tell there are many in need of my care."

But you haven't met any of them, Mal thought.

Percival, who had just entered the lobby, heard Dr. Forthright's directive issued from the phone. He walked over to the receptionist and explained that he'd seen the Maintenance Director leaving earlier and what he was doing.

"But that doesn't make any sense," the receptionist said. "Phillip is off today. He shouldn't be here."

Before Percival could respond, there was a sudden screech from Regina's office.

"No, no, no one touches my personal case! It contains personal medical supplies that you couldn't possibly understand how to use!"

The door opened and Mal walked backwards out of the office. Dr. Forthright was following her.

"As a matter of fact, Ms. Practiss, your services are no longer needed here. As an actual doctor, I don't need a nurse telling me how to run my community."

"Please! I'm sorry, Dr. Forthright. You can't fire me, it was an accident. You don't understand!"

"I understand all right. I understand that you've allowed your infirmity," here he glanced at Mal's leg, "to slow you down. I understand that you've neglected your duty to the residents. That you are as bad, or worse, than all of the other directors in this community. You will collect your things immediately!"

Millicent, Tina, and Percival watched Mal walk away, her head bowed, her shoulders racked with sobs.

Mal found Millicent and Tina waiting in the parking lot for her.

"Mal, we're so sorry," Tina said, her great big glasses magnifying the tears shimmering in her eyes.

"Yes, it's not right," said Millicent.

"What a terrible day," Tina said.

"It hurts. I'm a good director and I love the residents, but after I learned about your deceit, Millicent, I will never forgive you. Everything else pales in comparison. Maybe it's a good thing that I've been fired."

"Wh-why do you say that?" Tina asked. She looked nervously at Millicent, who was clutching her throat, her face shocked as if she'd just been slapped.

"Because as director, I'd made a promise to protect and care for every resident of Shady Bluff. But now I can focus on getting even with you, Millicent Trueworthy. You'd better watch your back."

She opened her car door and threw the box of office supplies in. Millicent jumped at the sound of the box hitting the passenger door and the contents spilling out.

"You shouldn't say such things, Mal," Tina said. "Millicent did what she thought was best. She was only trying to protect her son. Surely you understand that."

"I understand that Millicent kept the one thing he wanted most in this world away from him: to know his mother. I can't forgive her. And I won't forget," Mal said, turning her furious gaze on Millicent again.

"I..." said Millicent, but Mal slammed the car's door and the two women watched her speed out of the parking lot.

When they were back inside, Jonie was waiting for them. Before they could even share what Mal had told them, she held out a piece of paper. "I found another note."

With trembling hands Tina took the paper and unfolded it. "At midnight the clock will strike/ The way will all be cleared/ I took from you your husband/ Now I'll take the thing most dear."

Millicent frowned. "So, this person is taking credit for killing my son? But what could be dearer to Mal than him?"

Tina thought for a second. "To anyone who really knows Mal, the answer is nothing, she loved her husband more than anything. But it's obvious that whoever is leaving these little notes around is not only a cruel and cynical person, but also a bad writer who isn't half as clever as he thinks he is. The meaning can only be one thing: Mal's own life."

The women looked from one to another. "Someone's going to try to kill Mal at midnight tonight," Jonie said. "But we already assumed that. How does that help us?"

"I have an idea, but we need to look at all the letters Mal's received."

"That's going to be hard, considering that Mal just left the community for the last time," replied Jonie.

"We have to help Mal, I agree," said Millicent. "But first, we need to figure out what's happened to Cordelia. I have the sense that it's something terrible."

Cordelia woke in darkness. She felt herself, and whatever she was in, jostle, then slide forward. There was a scraping noise. *Someone's pushing me,* she thought, and the attack by the maintenance director came back to her. *What is he doing?*

She felt around, trying to determine what he had put her in: something wooden, and it smelled like mothballs. She had been placed inside on her side, her legs tucked. *My hope chest!*

She used her elbow to push against what she assumed to be the top, but it didn't budge. Meanwhile, she suddenly felt the end of the box dip and sway, balancing itself. *Oh no,* thought Cordelia. She imagined being pushed over the edge of the Perfidy Cliffs to shatter hundreds of feet below on the rocks, her body swept to sea and never found. So, when it tilted a bit further and then slid, she almost sighed with relief. The fall would have been a lot steeper than that. But then she felt the weight shifting and for a moment she was right side up before the chest fell forward. It made a sharp crack and Cordelia grunted as her weight readjusted itself forcefully.

Cordelia paused a moment, but there was no further movement. She didn't know if she should be quiet and still and wait to hear what was going on around her or if she should try to find a way out. Breathing slowly and reminding herself to stay calm, she decided that doing something was a better option than waiting for whatever that monster had in store for her.

She pushed as well as she could against the sides, but either she wasn't strong enough or she didn't have enough leverage to do anything. The wood didn't budge. She'd hoped that the cracking noise she heard had been enough to weaken the chest for her to push her way out. But this wasn't some cheap modern piece of particle board furniture.

As she tried to quell the panic rising in her, she suddenly heard the sound of something solid raining down upon her and then a loud *clump*.

Cordelia shook her head. It couldn't be. *He's burying me alive,* she realized. And that was when she started to scream.

To Be Continued...

Credits

Directors... Caitlyn Pec
Mary Robinson
Writers... Louise Anderson
Connie Capps
Howard Simmons

Acknowledgments

This story was created by, and for, the residents of Arrow Senior Living communities in multiple states, who found themselves seeking new creative outlets as the COVID-19 pandemic limited their ability to be with their friends, family, and neighbors.

We owe a large thank you to Chief Operating Officer Amanda Tweten who first said, "What if we wrote a book?" Thanks to the directors of the Resident Services departments (credited in chapters as the Director). We were thrilled to work with cover artist Kevin Tolibao and Dusan Arsenic, who provided the cover design.

Cast of Characters

Our story's heroes, Cordelia and Millicent, ere created by COO Amanda Tweten and writer oward Simmons. The rest of the characters were lded by residents as the story progressed. To ensure ontinuity as the story grew, residents created laracter sheets that provided following ommunities with information from which they could ork.

The following pages include character concepts y cover artist Kevin Tolibao and a little bit of iformation on some of the story's main players.

Cordelia Buttons

Age: 80
Widowed
No Children

Appearance: 5'4", slim, with gray hair that she pulls back into a bun. She likes to wear comfortable, but nice-looking clothes and prefers a sensible shoe. However, she doesn't mind dressing up now and then with a low heel. She doesn't wear jewelry often, save those occasions which also call for heels.

Bio: Cordelia is naturally curious. Her hero is Jessica Fletcher from "Murder, She Wrote." She can be sharp with those who try her patience, but she has a good heart and doesn't like to see people hurt, although she's willing to stretch the truth to get what she wants or to uncover a mystery.

Motives: The hero of our story, Cordelia wants to make sure that good wins out in the end and that the bad guys get what they deserve.

Millicent Trueworthy

Age: 76
Divorced
Two children

Appearance: Millicent prides herself on always putting her best foot forward. She's never seen without makeup, her hair done, and wearing something absolutely beautiful. Her one vice is her love of cigarettes. She can be found sometimes hiding outside sneaking one when she thinks no one is looking.

Bio: If her best friend, Cordelia, is "curious," Millicent is downright nosy and will do anything to make sure she's the center of attention – and knows all the gossip. This can get her into some serious trouble if she's not careful, especially as she has some secrets of her own she'd rather not get out.

Motives: Millicent wants to be the queen bee of Shady Bluff and will do whatever it takes. But she is also fiercely loyal to her friends and family.

Count Dandy Caruthers

Age: unknown
Married

Appearance: Count Dandy is a big man. Standing over 6', he exudes power and confidence. He is dressed as if from another time. He wears a monocle and has a small, pencil mustache. He dresses expensively, although that does not mean necessarily that he has taste.

Bio: The Count is, above all, *mysterious*. He keeps to himself and acts like he is above everyone. He likes to watch those around him, a sly look on his face as if he knows something about them that they'd rather he not. He likes shiny things: shiny shoes, shiny cufflinks, shiny knives...

Motives: The Count's motives are many and sometimes seemingly contradictory. But whatever his ultimate goal, it can't be good for the residents of Shady Bluff.

Percival Beauregard

Age: 79
Widowed
Two children

Appearance: Percival is short, bald, and a little overweight. He has a permanent 5 o'clock shadow. He's not always particular about his clothing or the state of them, always opting for comfort. He sometimes forgets to comb what little hair he has left.

Bio: Percival is almost too nice and eager to please once you get to know him. But he's also a bit gruff to those he doesn't know. He doesn't trust easily. As a retired police officer, he's always wanting to save the day. His idea of romantic wooing is turning up the machismo, which unfortunately doesn't have the desired effect on his unrequited love, Cordelia.

Motives: Percival wants Cordelia to fall madly in love with him, and for everyone else to see him as a hero.

Maxine Brûlée

Age: 48
Married
No children

Appearance: Tall and thin, Maxine is of Korean and French heritage. She has black hair with bangs and a mole under her left eye, which she sometimes scratches.

Bio: Quiet and soft-spoken, Maxine runs her kitchen efficiently and expects those who work with her to do their work well and with no drama. Some consider her demure to the point of mysteriousness. She talks little about herself and even less about her past.

Motives: Maxine wants to be left alone to do a good job and create excellent food for the residents. She wants only to earn a living and be happy. Unfortunately, at Shady Bluff, one's past is never truly left behind.

Countess Lily Rose Caruthers

Age: 60
Married
No children

Appearance: The Countess wears a bun as severe as her countenance. She is always dressed like she's going to a ball: lots of jewelry, lots of makeup. She is almost always wearing a pair of dark sunglasses, even inside. Woe to them she takes them off for – her withering gaze is rivaled only by Medusa.

Bio: Proper, poised, and hyperaware of her reputation, The Countess is demanding and snobbish. No matter the circumstances, she always carries herself with dignity.

Motives: The Countess Lily Rose wants her husband back at all costs, but not out of love. They both know too many of the other's secrets to ever part – except in death.

Printed in the USA
CPSIA information can be obtained
at www.ICGtesting.com
LVHW022226200823
755778LV00021B/109/J